Sud ... ut sou-
venirs ... plained
about t ... ade, or
too many mosquitoes. All I was thinking was that I'd never seen eyes so blue. They were the color of a deep ocean.

And they were smiling. As much as his mouth. But it was a crooked smile. One side a little higher than the other. Surrounded by dark stubble. Sexy stubble that matched the color of the hair falling forward over his brow.

"Hi," he said. His voice was a deep rumble.

I knew CCR policy was to greet each customer with a bright smile and a "Welcome to Coastal Campground Resorts. How can I help you?" But all I could manage was "Hi."

ALSO BY RACHEL HAWTHORNE

Caribbean Cruising

ISLAND GIRLS (AND BOYS)

RACHEL HAWTHORNE

AVON BOOKS
An Imprint of HarperCollins*Publishers*

Island Girls (and Boys)

Printed in the United States of America.
For information address HarperCollins Children's Books, a division of HarperCollins Publishers, 10 East 53rd St, 10022.
Library of Congress Catalog Card Number: 2004095708
ISBN 0-06-075546-6
First Avon edition, 2005

10 11 12 13 OPM 12 11 10 9 8

For Amanda Maciel
Whose guiding hand
made this story so much more fun!
Thanks for the
"unexpected journey."

ISLAND GIRLS

(AND BOYS)

CHAPTER 1

You're going to take an unexpected journey.

My horoscope for the day. Totally inaccurate. I was taking a journey all right, but it was one I'd been planning for months. I was exactly where I expected to be: crammed in the backseat of Amy's tiny car. Boxes were pressed against my side, a heavy sack of groceries rested on my knees, and assorted smaller items had been wedged around my feet, which were now numb.

This summer—the last before I started college—was going to be the absolute best of my life. I was embarking on my first summer of total independence, of saying good-bye to high school, good-bye to friends. The last—saying good-bye to friends—would be the most difficult, but

I planned to spend three months doing it, saying farewell to the best of the best: Chelsea Franklin and Amy Riley.

We were going to be together the entire summer—just the three of us. Working, living, playing. Saving up our memories for the days, weeks, and months ahead when only phone calls and an occasional weekend spent together would strengthen our bonds of friendship.

"How long before we're officially island girls?" Chelsea asked.

She was sitting in the front passenger seat with no more room than me. This was our third—and final—trip for the day. When we got to the island, we were staying for the summer.

"I think Jen and I already look like island girls," Amy said.

And we did. We were wearing shorts, tank tops, sneakers, and baseball caps. Amy's dark hair was held in place with a clip, and she'd pulled the long strands through the opening in the back of her cap. I'd done the same with my blond hair. Chelsea was also in shorts and a tank, but—

"Are you saying that I don't look like an

island girl?" Chelsea asked.

"You're too put together," Amy said.

Chelsea's black hair was cut short and fluffed out at various angles. She had deep blue eyes that were almost violet. She was tall, slender, and already totally tan, thanks to a gift certificate to a tanning salon that she'd received as a graduation present.

"This is called the ocean breeze look," Chelsea said indignantly. "I spent three hours working on it."

"That's my point," Amy said. "I don't think island girls spend a lot of time primping. They're more relaxed with their looks."

"And they're way more tan than us," I said. My skin was almost too pale to believe, almost as pale as my hair. I had to use X-Men-strength sunscreen, while Amy and Chelsea seldom worried if they forgot to use any at all. Two minutes in the sun and I was like a boiled lobster.

"I still can't believe we're doing this," Amy said.

It had been my scathingly brilliant idea: getting jobs on the island, staying at my grandparents' beach house over the summer.

A week ago, Grandma and Granddad had left for an extended vacation in Europe. Wouldn't need the house for several months. We could have it. As long as we agreed in writing to pay for the utilities, maintain the house, fix whatever broke, not have any wild parties—the last was stressed several times—and never make them regret leaving it in our care.

Not a chance were they going to regret it. We wanted this too much not to play by their rules.

Convincing our parents had been absolute torture: a series of arguments, pleadings, and promises. My mom had caved in first, narrowing her eyes and saying, "Jennifer Taylor, you'd better make darn sure that we don't come to regret our decision."

I didn't see how they could. It wasn't like we planned to do anything more than work and spend time together.

"I already miss Noah so much," Chelsea said with a low moan.

All right. So Chelsea also planned to miss Noah. Her boyfriend—when he was in town. Which wasn't very often.

Noah shared a dorm room with Chelsea's older brother. He'd come to town to visit her brother during Christmas break—and had ended up visiting with Chelsea more. He'd seen her several times since. I didn't know him well, but he seemed okay—except for the way that he always leaned on Chelsea like he didn't have the strength in his legs to hold himself up. Although I had to admit that it was cool to have a boyfriend who was already in college. Heck, it would be cool to have a boyfriend. I didn't and neither did Amy. But at least we didn't have to think about anyone except ourselves.

"You wouldn't have seen him that much anyway, Chels. It's not like he lives near you on the mainland," I said.

Not seeing him was the big objection she'd had to my idea. It had irritated me at the time. Still did. It was such a small inconvenience compared to the brilliance of my plan.

"Yeah, but if I'm working, and he comes to visit, *when will* I see him?"

I'd gotten us jobs at Coastal Campground Resorts where I'd worked last summer.

"There are twenty-four hours in the day," I

reminded her. "You'll work six. The rest are yours. How many would Noah need?"

"Every single one!"

"You're crazy."

"We're still defining our relationship, and I just don't know if I should have made this kind of major decision without considering him. Noah and I hadn't really talked much about our summer plans. Since you don't have a boyfriend, I don't expect you to understand."

Nice, Chels.

Chelsea and I were supertight, but since Noah had come into her life, she'd started acting like she thought she was the first girl in the history of the world to have a boyfriend.

"I've *had* a boyfriend," I pointed out. Over a year ago. But I had *had* a boyfriend. So I did know what it was like. "Besides, absence makes the heart grow fonder and all that."

"I never understood what that meant."

"By the end of the summer, he'll care more about you than he does now."

"I don't see how, if he never sees me." Chelsea threw up her hands.

"That's the whole point. Since he never sees

you, he dreams about you all the time so he misses you more and you become like a fantasy for him."

"I'd rather be a reality."

"Trust me. By the end of the summer, he'll want you way more than he does now."

"Speaking of summer, I can't believe we're going to be living completely alone," Amy said, gracefully changing the subject. She was the peacekeeper of our group.

"We've never even had a *weekend* completely alone together," she continued, "and we're going to have three whole months. I don't think it really hit me how alone we were going to be until we brought our first load of stuff over. Did anyone else get a really creepy feeling walking through the house? You know, like *isolation*?"

I knew we shouldn't have rented *Dawn of the Dead*. Amy is a quiet soul, a total nurturer. One of the reasons that she wants to be a veterinarian—she and animals can relate.

"Thank goodness!" Chelsea said. "I thought I was the only one who noticed. That house really creaks and moans."

"It's old, guys, that's all. Rustic. Quaint," I tried to reassure them.

"But what if there are like . . . dangers?" Amy asked.

"My grandparents have spent thirty summers there. It's completely safe. And the Coast Guard station is like a block down the road."

"I thought they just took care of stuff at sea," Chelsea said.

"If we call, the Coasties will come. They're not going to tell us to jump in a boat first."

"There's the bridge!" Amy shouted excitedly, just as she had every time that we'd neared it today.

Like she thought we couldn't look out the window and see the bridge that connected the mainland of Texas to this island. We lived an hour away, so it wasn't a complete mystery to us.

"Hope this old rattletrap can make it over the bridge one more time," Chelsea said.

"It's not a rattletrap," Amy said indignantly. "Besides, if you don't like riding in it, you should have said something sooner. We would have taken your car."

"I don't have a car," Chelsea said.

Amy gave her a satisfied smirk. "Exactly."

Amy's car was an ancient Gremlin her parents had bought to get her through the summer. Since it was our only mode of quick transportation—quick being a relative term—I wasn't complaining. I'd tied my bicycle to the roof when we took our first run so I'd have it handy for short trips and emergencies.

In a pinch, I figured I could even cycle to work. The island was a narrow strip of land about twenty miles long, with the bay on one side and the gulf on the other.

"It'll get us over the bridge," I said, hoping that it would. The bridge had a high arch because it had to allow room for boats and barges to move beneath it along the waterway.

We reached the arch. A sense of peace filled me as I took in the spectacular view, just before we started our descent. Palm trees lined the road that divided the island—the ocean was on one side, the coastal waterway on the other. So much sand and water. Sun and surf. Freedom!

In the distance, I saw Surf Town. It was a typical beach community, with small shops weathered by the wind and salt air. A few restaurants. The bold owners built right on the land. The not-so-bold, or, as I thought of them, the wise, built on stilts so they were protected from flooding when the tide unexpectedly rose more than normal.

And of course, along the beach were the usual touristy things: surfboard rentals, horse rentals, snow cone shacks.

Amy brought us to a lurching stop at the intersection. Straight ahead was the beach, but we weren't ready to go there yet. Soon, though. Very soon.

Amy turned right, and her little Gremlin puttered along. My grandparents' beach house was located at the far end, on the back side of the island.

"Do we need to stop at the convenience store?" Amy asked, as we neared a small store where the marquee boasted, LIVE BAIT!

"No," Chelsea said. "Let's just get to the house. My feet are going to sleep."

"Not *the* house," I corrected her. "*Our* house—"

"—for the summer!" we all finished at once.

"No parents!" Chelsea said.

"No brothers or sisters!" Amy said.

"No hassles!" I said.

"We can come and go when we want," Amy said.

"Not if your car breaks down," Chelsea teased.

"It's not going to break down," I said. "Be optimistic."

"I can't believe my parents agreed to this," Amy said.

"Why not?" Chelsea asked. "We'll all be going to college in the fall. They'll have no idea what we're doing then. So we're getting a head start."

"But we're not going to do anything they'd have a problem with, are we?" Amy asked.

Chelsea rolled her eyes. "Of course not. We'll be *good* girls." Although the way she said *good* made it sound like she meant the absolute opposite. That maybe she had plans to be a little bit bad. Then she laughed. "We're on our own!"

We reached the end of the island, and Amy turned toward the bay. We passed the Coast

Guard station and drove further along the sand-packed road.

Then the beach house came into view. White, wooden, it stood on stilts, surrounded on two sides by the bay. It had never looked more beautiful to me.

Amy brought the car to a halt beside the house.

"We're here!" she cried.

"Let's get everything inside," I said. "We have a lot of planning to do."

I opened the door and climbed out, my legs stiff and prickling as the blood rushed to my feet. I held the groceries in one arm, slung my backpack over my shoulder, and picked up another bag that had been at my feet.

The excitement grew intense as I led the way to the door. Although the main portion of the house was on stilts, there was a utility room on the ground where we went in.

At the top of the stairs was a short hallway. The door ahead of us led into the living room, where we'd dumped all our boxes during our previous trips. To the right was the kitchen. I went in and put the sacks on the counter.

All the blinds were open. I could look through the windows and see the dolphins jumping in the bay. I could hear the seagulls and the wind. I could smell the salt of the ocean and hear the roar of the surf.

I couldn't stop myself from bubbling up with exhilaration and anticipation as I faced my two best friends and flung my arms wide open.

"I hereby announce that as of this moment we're officially island girls! Let the best summer ever begin!"

CHAPTER 2

"Why do *you* get the main bedroom?"

I stared at Chelsea, unable to believe she'd asked. The room in question was the large bedroom on the main floor. Like the living room, it had a door that led out onto the balcony. It also had a private bathroom.

On the floor above us were three bedrooms and a shared bathroom in the hallway. Above that floor was a crow's nest, a small room open on four sides. You can see the entire island from up there, and the ocean and the ships on the horizon. But the crow's nest wasn't the issue.

"Because it's *my* grandparents' house?" I asked, not bothering to disguise my sarcasm. She was being ridiculous to even bring up the subject!

"This is supposed to be *our* house," Chelsea said.

"Well, yeah, but . . ." It had never occurred to me that I wouldn't have my grandparents' bedroom. It had a queen-size bed, a lovely antique dresser, a rocking chair, nightstands. The other rooms were nice, but they were for guests. The room in question had personality, history.

"This was my idea, the whole summer, working on the island, sharing the beach house—it was all my idea," I pointed out.

"So what? You want us thanking you for the next three months?"

I shook my head in disbelief. "Of course not."

"Then what? You think because it was your idea that you get to be in charge? That we have absolutely no say about how things are done?"

"Chels, we're all in charge. We're friends, we'll work together."

Chelsea ran her hands through her short hair in frustration. So much for her ocean breeze look. "But we're not working together. You've been bossing us around ever since we got here. Telling us where to put things in the kitchen—"

"Because I know where everything goes!"

"You know where everything goes when your grandparents are here. But they aren't here now. So why can't things be different? Why do they have to be the way they've always been or the way that *you* think they should be?"

"Because I've spent a lot of time thinking about how we would manage things while we're living here."

"And what if we don't want to do things the way you've decided?"

Then go home, I almost said. But that wasn't the answer, and it wasn't what I truly wanted. These were my best friends. We didn't always agree on everything, but we always managed to work through our differences.

"Then we need to talk about it," I admitted reluctantly.

"Exactly." Chelsea crossed her slender arms over her chest. She was supermodel flat. "What do you think, Amy?"

Amy had been quiet during the whole exchange. She dropped a Ping-Pong ball on the

Ping-Pong table on the far side of the room. It bounced, she caught it. Dropped it again, watched it bounce, caught it. She appeared to be more interested in the ball than in the argument.

"Maybe we should all sleep upstairs. There are three bedrooms up there. That way it would, like, be fair."

Chelsea looked at her as though she'd suggested driving her Gremlin up the stairs and parking it inside.

"But this bedroom is the largest, with the biggest bed, and its own bathroom! It's crazy not to use it."

"So I'll use it," I said.

"Not fair!"

"Chelsea, it's where my grandparents sleep."

"But they aren't here," she said again.

We'd barely gotten the car unloaded and the groceries put away when this discussion had started. All our boxes, all our things were scattered around the living room—which was also the TV room, the game room, the library. It was the center of the house, where everyone gathered during family get-togethers. I had a lot of memories of this room, but this was the first time that I could remember having an argument in here. I'd never realized how the room echoed.

"I'm not going to sleep upstairs," I said firmly. Wasn't that what you were supposed to do when you were living on your own? Take your stand and stick to it?

"Well, neither am I," Chelsea said. She plopped down on the couch, her arms still crossed, her nose in the air.

"Fine," I said sweetly. "You can sleep right there."

I picked up one of my boxes and started for the bedroom.

"Jennifer!" Chelsea jumped to her feet like someone had set a lit firecracker beneath her. "You can't just take the room."

"Maybe we could share the room," Amy suggested.

"Right!" Chelsea said. "Three empty bedrooms upstairs, and one crowded one down here. I don't think so."

"That's not what I meant," Amy said, still bouncing the ball.

I had this terrible urge to snatch it away from her. The constant clicking as it hit the table was really setting my nerves on edge.

"I meant," Amy continued, "that we could take turns."

"I don't want to get my room arranged and then have to switch rooms. I'll never feel moved in," Chelsea said.

"Then stop arguing and take a room upstairs," I told her.

"No."

"It won't be that bad to move our stuff around at the end of each month," Amy said. "Besides, it would be fun. We'd have different views all summer, and something to look forward to."

"The views aren't that different," Chelsea said. "Water. Water. Water."

"The views are very different," Amy said. "The bay, the far side of the island, and the Gulf. I wouldn't be able to choose my favorite, because each is special."

"When did you turn into Pollyanna?" Chelsea asked.

We were off to such a bad start. I couldn't believe it.

"No," I said with a sigh. "Amy is right. We can each have the large bedroom for a month."

"I get it first," Chelsea announced.

"Could you be any more self-centered?" I asked.

"I'm not self-centered, I just want it first."

"We could play Ping-Pong for it," Amy suggested. Her brown eyes were watching us intensely, and I knew this continual arguing was making her uncomfortable. You'd think she'd be used to it, growing up with four brothers.

"Not Ping-Pong," I said. I walked to the bookshelves. I knelt, opened the doors in the lower portion, and pulled out the Monopoly game.

"Not Monopoly," Chelsea whined.

"Not Monopoly," I agreed. "Just the dice."

I took them out of the box and carried them to the Ping-Pong table. "We each get one roll. Highest roll gets it the first month, second highest the second month, and the lowest gets it last. Agreed?"

Chelsea and Amy exchanged glances, then both nodded. Thank goodness. This was *so* not the way that I'd planned to start the summer. I handed Chelsea the dice. "You can go first."

She threw a five and a four.

Amy threw a two and one. She would definitely have the room the last month. No way was I going to throw something lower than a three. What I really wanted was to have the room first, because I figured by the end of the month everyone would be settled and no one would want to switch. A little tricky thinking there, but I was certain that was the way it would go.

"Come on double six," I whispered as I blew on the dice. Shook them in my palm. Blew on them again.

"Come on already," Chelsea said. "Throw 'em."

I shook, blew, tossed them.

Snake eyes. Two.

The disappointment overwhelmed me. I couldn't believe how very much I'd wanted to start my summer in that bedroom. Instead, I would end the summer with it. All right. So be it. I could be a good sport about this. I really could.

I went into the kitchen, took the complimentary bait-and-tackle calendar that my granddad got each year from the sporting goods store off the wall, grabbed a pen, and walked back into the living room. Chelsea was already moving her boxes into the room I wanted.

"Chelsea, come here."

"I won."

"I know you did, but I want us to agree when the room switching will take place." I wrote her name on the square for today. "Thirty days from now"—I lifted the calendar page—"Amy will move into the room."

I wrote her name on the designated date. "Thirty days later, I'll move into it." I looked at them. "Does everyone agree?"

They nodded.

"Initial the calendar," I ordered.

"Who put you in charge?" Chelsea asked.

"I just don't want anyone saying that she didn't understand how we were going to work this."

"She's right," Amy said. "We're supposed to work together."

We initialed the calendar, the pictures of

various open-mouthed fish bearing witness.

"Great!" Chelsea said. "Let's finish moving in."

She moved across the living room and into the bedroom with a lithe catlike walk that came with her willowy height.

"My mom told me to expect that we'd have to make some adjustments," Amy said to me. "It's kinda like being married."

"It's nothing like being married. Married people don't argue about which bedroom to sleep in."

"She snores. Do you really want to sleep with her?"

I couldn't stop myself from smiling. "No. I just . . . whenever I thought of the summer, I saw myself in that room."

"You'll have it in two months."

"Right."

But after the rocky start, I wondered if in two months, I'd still have my friends.

CHAPTER 3

I'd attended a funeral that was more joyful than we were as we carted our boxes to our individual rooms. Even the song I heard Chelsea humming when I came downstairs for another load sounded sad.

I stood in the living room, looking through the open blinds. The sun was going down. I found that sad as well. Our first big night on our own, away from our parents, the start of our exciting independent island girl summer . . . it was nothing like I expected.

I was beginning to accept that maybe I'd been selfish to expect to have my grandparents' bedroom all summer. It *was* the best in the house. Without a doubt. But Chelsea and Amy were the best, too. We didn't have to agree on everything, but I wanted our arguments to be about something that truly mattered—not a silly room. I didn't want to be sad or missing my friends before we'd even left for college!

It was frightening to think that in only three months, I'd be separated from them. We were going to different universities in the fall. This summer was our last chance to be totally devoted to one another, to share our dreams, to start preparing for the bright future that all the graduation speeches talked about.

"What are we doing?" I shouted. "Why are we unpacking while the sun is still out? This is insane! Let's go walk on the beach!"

Amy bounded down the stairs, laughing. "I was just thinking the same thing."

"Me, too," Chelsea said as she came out of my grandparents' bedroom.

Be nice, I told myself. It was *her* bedroom, not my grandparents'. For a month. She was coming out of *her* room.

I grabbed the keys out of my backpack and stuffed them into the front pocket of my shorts. We each had a key to the house—not that I thought we'd ever be separated, but something might come up. Like one of us walking on the beach, while the other two were napping or . . . well, anything. "Be prepared" was my motto.

Although I certainly hadn't been prepared for Chelsea to want the bedroom that I wanted. But this was also a summer of learning to adjust. I'd be sharing a dorm room with a complete stranger. Surely I could share a beach house with my friends.

"Let's go!" I exclaimed.

We turned for the door. A cell phone chirped out a rendition of the musical score from *Jaws*.

"Hold on, that's mine," Chelsea said. She ran back to her bedroom.

"Hi!" I heard her exclaim. "I'm so glad you called."

She appeared in the doorway. "Just a sec," she said into the phone. She looked at us, pleading for understanding with her violet eyes. "It's Noah. I'll catch up with you."

Then she disappeared back into the bedroom.

I looked at Amy. "I guess it's just you and me, girlfriend."

We headed down the stairs. I opened the door, and we stepped outside. I was hit by the smell of the sea. Not completely pleasant, but not totally icky. I could smell fish and salt and brine.

Amy picked up an old metal bucket that was sitting by the door.

"What's that for?" I asked.

"I want to decorate my room with seashells. That's about the only souvenir I'll be able to afford this summer."

"Your money might go farther than you think. I've worked up a budget for us. But I'll wait until tomorrow to show you. I don't want Chelsea going ballistic because I made a plan."

I was expecting to major in business. I loved figuring out budgets, working with columns of numbers, especially when those numbers translated into money.

"We're all in this together," Amy said. "We have to keep things fair. And you're the one who aced math."

"Still, we can talk about it tomorrow. And how we want to divide the chores. There's probably a hundred things I haven't thought of."

"Relax, Jen. Everything will be fine."

I wanted it to be. I really did. But I couldn't

help feeling responsible. After all, it had been my idea.

I shoved my hands into the front pockets of my shorts and started walking along the sand-packed road toward the beach. Amy was walking beside me, the bucket swinging, occasionally clanging as it bumped against her leg. She was the shortest of the group, so I shortened my strides so she could keep up more easily. It was a habit I fell into naturally.

I could see the sand dunes in the distance. Beyond them, the brown waves rolled onto the shore. Here the water wasn't blue and clear, like I'd heard it was on tropical islands. Far out in the distance, it looked blue, but near the shore it was brown. Not dirty or polluted. Just brown.

"I can look out my window and see the dolphins jumping in the bay. How cool is that?" Amy asked.

Amy had graciously taken the bedroom that had two single beds in it. It faced the bay. I'd taken the bedroom that faced the ocean—mostly because it had a double bed, while the last bedroom had bunk beds. Bunk beds felt too much like summer camp.

"Very cool," I said. "Whenever I stay here, I like to leave the windows open and have the breeze blow the curtains. It's so peaceful."

The house had air-conditioning. But unless the day was really hot, I preferred not using it. Which would also give us a lower electric bill.

"It was so nice of your grandparents to let us have the house," she said.

I realized that it was the first time anyone had actually acknowledged my grandparents' generosity.

"They're really nice people," I told her. "Every time I walk into that house, I feel like they're hugging me. I know that sounds silly—"

"No, it doesn't. I feel the same way when I go to my grandma's. There's just something about a house when people have lived in it for a long time. Like it has absorbed their personalities or something."

"I've always loved spending time out here, Amy. It's peaceful and calm. Don't you think it's relaxing?"

"Definitely. There's just something about the salt air and breeze. Makes me feel like we'll be on a perennial vacation."

"That feeling will go away tomorrow, though, when we start working."

We trudged up the sand dunes and over to the sandy spot that was the main area of the beach. I could only see a few cars down the way. It was getting late. The sun was going down. The weekend was ending. Like us, most people had to work tomorrow.

I slipped off my sandals and walked to the water's edge. I removed my cap, pulled my hair loose, and let the breeze blow the strands around my face. Now I *could* smell rotting fish.

Amy was picking up seashells and putting them in her bucket. "Some of these are so pretty," she said. "I think I'll use them to make a shadowbox display so I'll remember this summer. I'll make each of us one as a souvenir."

"You might want to check with Chelsea first, get a vote. Don't want her to think you've taken control of the souvenir decisions."

I didn't mean to sound petty, but I guess I was still bothered that Chelsea had thought I was being bossy.

"She's the baby in her family. She's used to being spoiled."

"I never really noticed that before."

"You're the oldest in the family. Being in charge comes natural to you."

"And you're the middle child," I pointed out.

She studied a shell before dropping it into her bucket. "Right. The mediator."

We'd all been in the same psych class our senior year.

"Chelsea probably sees this summer as being a long slumber party," Amy added.

"I'd sorta thought that, too," I admitted. "A long slumber party with responsibilities."

"Which you've already divided between us," she said, before bending down to pick up another shell.

"Well, yeah! But we can discuss things. Nothing is written in stone except that when my grandparents come back, they shouldn't be able to tell that anyone lived in their house over the summer."

Amy looked up at me from her crouched position and held something out. "Do you know what kind of shell this is?"

It was thin, ridged. Nothing special. "Seashell?"

She laughed. Amy had a fun laugh that made you want to laugh along with her.

"Hey, guys!" Chelsea was rushing toward us. She came to a quick stop, laughing and breathing hard. "I was afraid I'd waited too long, and I wouldn't be able to find you."

"How's Noah?" Amy asked.

"Missing me. I didn't think I'd feel so isolated. The only way I can see him is if he comes here."

"But that would be true even if you were at your house," Amy said. "He lives hundreds of miles away from there, too."

"I know. It's hard to explain what it's like to someone who's never had a boyfriend," Chelsea said.

Okay, Chelsea and her boyfriend comments were getting seriously old, but I so did not want to get irritated at her over something else.

Amy apparently took no offense at Chelsea's statement. She laughed. "I know all about boys, Chelsea. In case you've forgotten, I have four brothers. The last thing I want is another boy in my life."

"What about you, Jen?" Chelsea asked. "Don't you miss having a boyfriend?"

"I'm going to be too busy this summer with work and living on my own. I'm with Amy on this."

"It's going to be a good summer, isn't it?" Chelsea asked.

"The best," I assured her.

"I'm sorry I got all bent about the bedroom," Chelsea said.

"Sorry I came across as being bossy. We're just going through a period of adjustment."

"Yeah, right. Everything is going to be totally cool once we get settled in."

"Oh, y'all, look at the sunset. Isn't it gorgeous?" Amy asked.

It really was. The sun splashed vibrant orange, purple, and pink across the darkening sky.

I hooked my arms through Chelsea's and Amy's. I suddenly felt small, insignificant, and scared. A summer on our own was a big step.

"You're my best friends in the whole world," I told them.

We hugged one another, and I knew they felt the same way.

CHAPTER 4

I loved being on the island as dawn hovered, not quite there yet, still only a promise in the dark. There was something magical and romantic about it.

I crawled out of bed and powered up my laptop. I'd set it up the night before on a little rickety desk that I think my grandma picked up at a garage sale. I liked to start each day by checking out my horoscope online—one of my little guilty pleasures. It seemed contradictory for someone as business-minded as I was to turn to the stars for advice, but I liked seeing how close the predictions were.

Today's was a bit disconcerting, though. *An important relationship will not go in the direction you had hoped.*

What did that mean?

It had to mean a bad direction, because I would only hope for a good direction. So was I going to have a falling out with someone? With whom? Chelsea? Amy? My employer? My summer list of important relationships was short.

The house was quiet as I crept down the stairs in the dark. I went into the kitchen and flipped on the light.

For some reason, I was always more hungry on the island. Maybe it was the fresh air. I opened a can of cinnamon rolls, arranged them in a baking dish, and put them in the oven.

I made a cup of green tea and took it to the table. The kitchen didn't have a traditional table. It had a booth set against the window. I opened the blinds. I could see the lights twinkling on the mainland. The sky was beginning to lighten. I crossed the room, turned out the light, and returned to the table. Sitting, I lifted my feet to the opposite bench and cleared my mind of horoscopes. I heard a foghorn blast.

This is the life, I thought. Going to bed when I wanted. Getting up when I wanted. Cooking what I wanted to eat for breakfast. Every decision mine to make.

Another foghorn sounded. It was such a lonely isolated sound. I could see the silhouette of a barge moving sluggishly through the canal between the island and the mainland.

The timer went off. I took the rolls out of the oven and slathered all of the icing on half of them. I went back to the table, the aroma of cinnamon wafting around me.

The sky was growing lighter. I could see four sleek, beautiful dolphins, leaping out of the water.

What a fantastic way to begin the day! It promised to be the best.

I'll also have to add a five-dollar pain-in-the-butt charge to your bill.

That's what I was *thinking* as I smiled at the customer standing in front of me at the campground registration counter. What I actually *said*—with a sickeningly sweet smile—was, "Enjoy your stay with us, Mr. Warner!"

With a grunt, he picked up his copy of the registration form that I'd filled out for him. He trudged to the door and opened it. The bell above it tinkled. As the door closed, I could hear Mr. Warner still grousing about the absence of shade trees.

Hello! I wanted to shout after him. *We're on the beach! Fun, sun, sand! It comes with the territory! If you wanted shade, you should have gone camping in the woods!*

But I didn't shout at him. I kept smiling.

This morning, after Chelsea and Amy joined me for breakfast, we'd discussed our budget for the summer. We were making minimum wage, only working thirty-six hours a week. We didn't have to pay rent. But we did have to pay for food, utilities, our cell phones, and gas to get us back and forth to work, since the campground was on the opposite side of the island from where we were living. And, of course, we wanted to be able to party a little.

Which was the reason that I'd smiled at Mr. Warner instead of telling him to drive his thirty-four-foot travel trailer into the gulf. Honestly, sometimes I didn't understand campers. Camping to me was a tent, in the wild, away from civilization, roughing it.

Although I probably shouldn't talk. Working

at Coastal Campground Resorts was actually the closest I'd ever come to camping. I'd given Chelsea and Amy the grand tour when we arrived this morning. Then Mrs. Plackette had given us our assignments and our uniform, which we dutifully changed into: tan cargo shorts, a red polo shirt with the CCR logo, and a name tag.

She and her husband owned and managed the campground. What she lacked in height she made up for with energy. Even I had a hard time keeping up with her.

The main building where Chelsea and I worked housed the registration area and a couple of cash registers at the front. But most of the building was a store that stocked just about anything campers and beach buffs might need: groceries, tackle equipment, snorkeling equipment, souvenirs.

I could look through the floor-to-ceiling plate glass windows and see the Beach Hut—the snack bar and arcade—where Amy was working. Campers parked between the two buildings while they came in to register. Mr. Warner was just now pulling his monster trailer through so he could take it to his designated site.

And with no one in line behind him, I had to return to the grunge work. You'd think working at a registration desk was easy, but I wasn't paid to stand around and wait for customers. I crouched beside a large box. Our summer souvenirs had arrived. I had to verify that we'd been sent exactly what we'd ordered. This box was supposed to have forty-eight "Beach LVR" T-shirts. I had counted thirty-six when I heard the bell tinkle.

I shoved myself to my feet . . . and stopped breathing.

Suddenly I wasn't thinking about souvenirs or camp guests who complained about too much sand, not enough shade, or too many mosquitoes. All I was thinking was that I'd never seen eyes so blue. They were the color of a deep ocean.

Framed by long, dark lashes, they were set beneath thick, dark eyebrows. And they were smiling. As much as his mouth—which had a crooked smile. One side a little higher than the other. Surrounded by dark stubble. Sexy stubble that matched the color of the hair falling forward over his brow.

"Hi," he said.

His voice was a deep rumble that made me think of sharing secrets in the night.

Somewhere in the back of my mind I knew CCR policy was to greet each customer with a bright smile and a "Welcome to Coastal Campground Resorts. How can I help you?" But all I could manage was "Hi."

Totally wrong. I hoped no one reviewed the security tapes later.

"We were wondering how much it costs to camp here," he said.

We. We. We?

I snapped to attention, broadened my vision, and noticed the guy standing beside him. But his blond hair and brown eyes barely registered with me. I turned my attention back to Blue Eyes. "What kind of vehicle?"

"Motorcycle."

I shook my head. I'd been asking about recreational vehicle. RV. Camping vehicle. "What do you sleep in?"

"Our boxer shorts," his friend said.

Blue Eyes laughed. "Come on, Zach. That's

not what she was asking."

He dropped his gaze to my chest. I wondered if he was hearing the hard thudding of my heart and wanted to watch when it burst through my ribs. He lifted his gaze back to me.

"Jennifer—"

My name tag. He'd been reading my name tag.

"—we have a tent."

I swallowed hard, cleared my throat, and went into sales speak. "Uh, for a tent, we have several options. We have the actual campsites that are blacktopped. You could park your motorcycle on the blacktop and pitch your tent on the sand between the sites. You'd have access to an electrical outlet and a water hookup there. It's twenty dollars a night."

He grimaced. "Ouch. You said several options. Let's skip right to the cheapest."

"That would be the beach." And truly the only other option. I couldn't figure out why I'd said "several" when there were really only two: paved campsite or beach.

"How much is that?" he asked.

"Actually, the beach is free."

"That's what we want," Zach said.

"Not so fast," Blue Eyes said. "What's the catch?"

"It's ten dollars if you want to use the camp facilities."

"Does that include the showers?"

I nodded.

"What else does that ten bucks get us?"

"The pool, mini-golf, shuffleboard—"

"Yeah, like I want to spend time playing shuffleboard with someone's grandpa before I go into the army," Zach said.

"Are you going into the army?" I asked Blue Eyes.

"At the end of the summer. We're camping along the coast until we leave."

"That's awesome."

"Yeah, so far it's been great. If we camp on the beach and pay our ten bucks, when do we have to stop using the shower?" he asked.

I was a little disappointed that he'd gotten right back to the business at hand, when I wanted to know more about him. It was so strange, because I was never curious about the campers. But then most of them weren't this hot.

"Noon tomorrow," I told him.

He looked over at his friend. "I really want to use that shower."

"If we pay our money tonight," Zach said, "can we stay camped out there tomorrow night if we don't pay tomorrow?"

I nodded. "Like I said, the beach is free. You just can't use the facilities."

"Okay," Blue Eyes said. "Where do I sign?"

I handed him a registration form. "Just fill that out, and I'll give you a passkey that'll get you into the showers."

"Cool."

I watched as he wrote in the information. His name was Dylan Nelson. His address was in Dallas. When he was finished, I took his registration form and his ten dollars. I felt guilty taking his money because it sounded like he didn't have much, like he was watching his budget as closely as I was.

"I hope you'll enjoy your visit with us," I said as I handed each of them a passkey.

"Oh, I'm sure we will," Dylan said.

"How long are you planning to stay?" I asked.

Dylan gave me a devastatingly sexy smile. "Definitely longer than I'd originally planned."

CHAPTER 5

I watched as the guys got on their motorcycles, visible through the window. One of the cycles had a tiny trailer behind it, which I figured held their tent. They took off toward the beach, leaving me wishing I could follow.

"Jennifer?"

My heart nearly jumped into my throat, strangling my startled screech. I spun around. Mrs. Plackette was standing there, a speculative look on her face. Her graying hair was pulled back in a bun.

"Is everything all right?" she asked.

"It's awesome, but I was thinking maybe I should take a park run."

She nodded. "Probably a good idea. Make sure everyone is where they're supposed to be."

"Great. I'll see to it and then finish counting the souvenirs when I get back."

I grabbed the clipboard that dangled from a hook beneath the huge map of the campground that was hanging on the wall behind the counter. The sites were marked: those rented, those not. A couple of times a day, we did a park run, clipboard in hand, which had a miniature campground map on it.

We would mark the sites that were occupied and then come back to compare so we could make sure everything matched up. Sometimes people tried to sneak in without paying, but it usually took only one encounter with Mr. P—who was built like a tank—for people to decide that registering first was a smart move.

Since I'd worked here last summer, I knew most of the rules and what needed to be done. Mrs. P had told me that I would be the unofficial assistant manager. Wasn't sure why it couldn't be official, but whatever.

I had just gone around the counter into the store area when she spoke again. "Jennifer?"

I looked back at her. "Yes, ma'am?"

"A word of advice. Campers never stay long,

no matter how cute they are. We don't need any broken hearts over the summer."

Was I that easy to read? Had she been standing there when I registered our latest guests?

"A broken heart is not in my plans," I reassured her.

"It never is," she said. "Don't be gone too long."

"Yes, ma'am."

Checking out the campground was hot work, so I stopped by the cooler at the back of the store to grab a bottle of water. I opened the door and welcomed the blast of frigid air that Chelsea was cursing. She was inside, wearing a coat, and placing drinks on the shelves.

"I'm going on a park run," I yelled into the cooler.

She rubbed her nose. "Lucky you. You forgot to tell me that I'd be spending my summer in Antarctica."

I laughed. "Only a couple of times a day."

"That's a couple of times too many."

"You'll get used to it. Later!" I said and closed the door.

The building had doors on both sides of it that led to the outside. The main door faced the area where people drove through with their campers. The back door faced the marina. I went out the back door and walked to the marina where the golf cart was parked.

"Hey, Mr. P!" I called out.

He waved from the dock, then went back to looking into a bait well where live shrimp were waiting to be dipped out and handed over to anxious fishermen. The marina had everything the store didn't: gasoline pumps, bait, a boat ramp, and a large blacktop area off to the side where people parked after backing their boats into the water.

In addition to being on the far side of the narrow island, the campground was on the back side, the bay side. There was an inlet that formed a lagoon. It led into the bay, and the bay—between the island and a jutting portion of mainland—led into the Gulf of Mexico.

I climbed into the golf cart, started it up, and took off. I drove around the lagoon side of the campground, marking the few sites that were occupied. Then I headed toward the other side, driving along the far edge that ran along the length of the bay.

I stopped when I neared the area where Dylan and Zach were putting up their tent. I didn't really have a plan. I just felt like I had to do . . . *something*.

I walked between two empty blacktop sites that I knew would have trailers on them by the weekend. Then I stepped onto the beach, loose sand shifting beneath my feet as I made my way to where the guys were.

Dylan stopped working as I neared. "Did we pick a spot that's off limits?"

"Oh, no, you're fine." Did he think I was the campground police or something? I nodded toward the tent. "I'm just amazed. You could give lessons on putting up a tent. I've never seen one go up so fast."

Okay. I'd never actually watched one go up. It wasn't exactly on my list of the top hundred-and-one things to see before I died.

"The quicker we get it up, the more time we have to explore," Dylan explained.

"And find babes," Zach said. He leaned over slightly, like someone who realizes that the movie camera isn't focused on him and wants to be in the picture. So all the camera picks up is his head and stretched neck. I couldn't decide if he was funny or pathetic.

"I can't help you there," I said. And it occurred to me that if Zach was all about finding babes, maybe Dylan was, too. And maybe I shouldn't show any interest in him, because like Mrs. P had said—he wouldn't stay long.

I lifted my clipboard. "Well, I'd better get back to work. I just wanted to make sure you were getting settled in okay."

"You do that for all the campers?" Dylan asked.

"As much as possible," I lied. "We try to make everyone feel welcome."

"So we're just part of the crowd?"

I flung out my arms. "Do you see a crowd?"

He laughed. It was a really nice laugh. "Guess not. So what do you recommend for two guys passing through? Is Surf Town a happening place?"

I suddenly felt really dull. Every time I'd come to the island with my parents, I'd built sand castles, sunbathed, and played in the ocean.

Last night, we'd eaten pizza. Not very exciting. We hadn't done all the things we'd planned and talked about for months. We hadn't partied. We hadn't gone clubbing. We hadn't become absorbed in the island culture. We'd unpacked.

"There are some clubs," I said.

"Which is the best?"

I hadn't a clue. But I didn't want to admit that. "They all have something different to offer."

"We like different," Zach said.

"How long have you been camping?" I asked inanely, trying to turn the conversation onto familiar ground.

Dylan shifted his stance. "A little over a week. We started right at the Louisiana border, and we're working our way down to Mexico."

"What do you do at night?"

"Are you issuing an invitation?"

I suddenly wished the sand beneath my feet would open up and swallow me whole. I wasn't a complete stranger to flirting, but this was way out of my league. "No, just curious. Making conversation."

"Well, then, for conversation's sake, it depends on where we are. If we're near a town, we check it out, party, meet people . . . have fun. If a town isn't close, we just build a fire, watch the stars come out."

Watching the stars come out with Dylan sounded to me like the most exciting thing a girl could ever do. I wanted to stay and talk with him, but my dependability buzzer went off.

"I really do have to get back to work," I said.

"Maybe we'll see you later."

"Maybe."

I trudged back to the cart, climbed on, drove through another section of sites, then circled back around, driving by the bathhouse, then the pool. I pulled to a stop in front of the Beach Hut. I went into the building. No one was in the arcade area, but lights still flashed on the machines lining the side walls. Between the walls were two pool tables.

I strolled on through to the snack bar. A few metal tables and chairs were scattered throughout the area. Stools lined the actual snack bar.

"Hey, girlfriend!" I shouted to Amy.

She was behind the counter, her elbows resting on top, her chin in her palms.

"I am bored out of my freaking mind!" she

lamented. "I haven't had a single customer."

"Wait for the weekend," I told her. "We'll be full by then, and you'll wish you didn't have any customers."

"I hope you're right, because I need something to make the day go by quickly."

"Trust me. The days will go faster than you can imagine."

"If you say so."

"Did you happen to see the motorcycles out there?" The front of the building was all glass, giving her a view of the campers coming through.

"Yeah. Why?"

"They belong to a couple of hotties who are putting up a tent on the beach."

"So things might get interesting around here."

"It's a possibility."

CHAPTER 6

Our usual shift was ten until four, but with the shortage of campers, Mrs. P cut us loose at three. The evening crew would arrive soon, and it was slow enough that she could handle things until then. She had Amy close down the snack bar. A metal fencelike barrier slid from one side of the building to the other, keeping people out of the snack area while letting them play in the arcade area.

We climbed into Amy's car. Me in the back, because I rode in the front on the way to work. Even without all the boxes and bags, it was still cramped.

"What are we going to do when we get home?" Amy asked.

"Change into bathing suits and hit the beach,"

Chelsea answered. She looked over her shoulder at me. "Right?"

She was asking me?

"Sure. I'd like to be a little tan by the end of summer. If I start now with just a bit of time in the sun each day, I should be able to spend more time outside without burning. Peeling skin is the absolute worst."

"Do we get a discount on things we buy in the campground store?" Chelsea asked.

"Yeah, but everything is more expensive on the island," I said. "Even with a discount. Maybe we should plan on going back to the mainland once a week for major shopping."

"We could make a night of it," Amy said. "Catch a movie or whatever."

"We'd need to go to the matinee," I said. "When tickets are cheaper."

Chelsea turned around in her seat, straining against the seatbelt to face me. She moved her sunglasses down her nose so she could peer at me with her piercing violet eyes. "Why are you so worried about every penny?"

"Because we have bills to pay, and our parents

aren't here to hand over a twenty if we need something."

"So we go see them if we run out of money. It's not like they're in another country."

I wanted to pound my head against the back of her seat. "I'm trying to prove that I can live on my own."

"Me, too," Amy said. "No emergency trips to our families."

With a heavy sigh, Chelsea pushed her sunglasses into place and twisted back around. "Okay. It just seems like undue hardship to me."

"Think of it as an adventure."

"An adventure in poverty," Chelsea said. "Doesn't really appeal, you know?"

"I think it'll emphasize our resourcefulness," Amy said.

She turned the car onto the sand-packed road that led to our house. Past the Coast Guard station. One of the Coasties waved at us. We waved back.

"Think they'd give us a ride in the Coast Guard boat?" Chelsea asked.

"I doubt it," I said. "But the campground

rents sailboats at the marina. We can use them for free if they're available."

"Those little things bobbing in the water?" Chelsea asked.

"They hold two people. I took one out last summer. They're fun, and pretty easy to handle."

"I'd rather have a big boat with lots of guys around who know what they're doing," Chelsea said.

"Who's here?" Amy asked.

I looked through the windshield. I could see a black truck parked near the house. A guy stepped out.

Chelsea released an earsplitting squeal. "It's Noah!"

She had the door open before Amy brought the car to a stop. She leaped out, ran to Noah, and threw her arms around his neck. His went around her waist. And then they were kissing like they'd stepped into make-out central.

Amy twisted around and looked at me. "Well, this is a surprise."

"No kidding."

"You'd think she'd tell us if she knew he was coming."

"You'd think."

Amy turned the car off. "She had to know. Otherwise, he wouldn't have known where to find us."

"Yeah."

"I guess she didn't *have* to tell us he was coming."

"No. But she didn't *have* to keep it a secret either."

"Too bad he didn't come yesterday. We could have used his truck to get everything here in one trip."

"Yeah, it would've been nice," I said.

We climbed out of the car, slamming the doors extra loudly to give warning that we were on our way.

But Chelsea and Noah were caught in a lip-lock that seemed to know no end. I didn't want to be rude. I cleared my throat. "Hey, Noah!"

He pulled back. "Hey, Jen. Hey, Amy."

He was really cute. Tall and lean, with dark hair and eyes.

Chelsea wrapped her arm around his waist, and he anchored her up against his side. Like he'd topple over if she weren't there.

"This is a cool place," he said.

"You're going to love it," Chelsea said. "Come on. I'll show you my bedroom."

Chelsea showed him "her" bedroom with the door closed.

After nearly half an hour, Amy and I got tired of waiting for them to emerge from their cocoon. We changed into our bathing suits and headed out.

The beach was totally open and almost deserted except for a couple of little kids running around near one of the other beach houses. We laid our towels on the sand. I'd slathered a huge amount of suntan lotion on my body before I'd left the house. So I sat on the towel, reached into my beach bag, and pulled out a romance novel. I rolled over onto my stomach, rested on my elbows, pushed my sunglasses farther up the bridge of my nose, and started reading.

I was completely lost in the story when Amy asked, "Do you think they're in love?"

I pulled myself back to reality and looked around. I couldn't figure out who she was talking about. Finally I looked at her. "Who?"

"Chelsea and Noah."

"Sure looked like it."

"I knew they were dating, but I didn't realize it was serious enough that he'd come down here to see her."

"Looked pretty serious," I admitted.

"What's he doing for the summer?"

I shrugged. "I don't know. I think he actually lives somewhere near Fort Worth. Chelsea hasn't told me a lot about him."

Amy grinned. "Except that he's hot."

I grinned back. "He is that."

"Does it bother you not to have a boyfriend?" she asked.

Her brow was furrowed. Even though she was wearing sunglasses, too, I could see that she was serious about the question. Her brown eyes were lost behind the shades but I could feel her studying me, and I knew my answer was important.

"Sometimes, sure. But I figure when we go off to college, we're going to meet so many new people. By Christmas, we'll both have boyfriends. That's why I wanted to spend this summer with you and Chelsea. Just the three of us. When we go off to different schools in the fall, our lives will change so much."

"But we won't change," Amy said.

"Of course not. Just everything around us."

"I'm cool with that. But sometimes I get scared. I want to hold on to what we have, but it seems like parts of it are already going away. I mean, look, Chelsea isn't here."

"Noah will leave soon, and then she will be."

"You're right. I'm worrying for nothing." She unclipped her hair, ran her fingers through it, then re-clipped it. "Those guys you mentioned earlier, the bikers—"

"They're not really bikers. I don't think. Not like Hell's Angels or anything."

"Whatever. It just got me to thinking. I thought this was going to be the summer of us girls."

"It is, but I didn't think we'd have a full guy embargo. After all, we want to party some, and that's more fun with guys around."

"I guess."

"I'm not going to get serious about anyone," I assured her. "Especially a camper who's just passing through."

"Even if he's Orlando Bloom hot?"

"Not even then, because campers don't stay." Mrs. P's warning echoed through my mind. Not that I'd really needed it. I'd met enough guys last summer to know that flirting with the campground employees was just a game for campers, a part of summer fun.

"Hey, girlfriends!"

We both looked over and saw Chelsea walking toward us.

"There, see," I told Amy. "Noah has left already."

Chelsea knelt in front of us. "Since Noah's here, let's go out tonight to celebrate."

Okay. So Noah hadn't left.

"To celebrate what?" Amy asked.

"Anything! Everything! The beginning of summer. Our independence. The fact that I'm madly in love!"

"I'll have to count my change first," I said, grinning. "See what I can afford."

Chelsea laughed. "I'll treat."

"No way. But you're right. We need to celebrate the beginning of . . . everything."

CHAPTER 7

We ended up going to the Sandpiper, a restaurant in Surf Town right on the beach.

We sat outside at a table on the wooden deck. I watched the waves lapping at the shore, and tried not to notice the way Chelsea kept sneaking a sip of Noah's beer whenever the waitress wasn't around.

"So your grandparents aren't going to check up on you?" Noah asked.

He had his chair tipped back against the railing. Totally relaxed. Yet his arm was slung around Chelsea, holding her against his side. I wondered if she was going to put her plate on his chest so she could stay in that position to eat once our food arrived.

"They trust us," I told him.

"Totally cool. So you can do whatever you want?"

"Sure. Within reason."

"Awesome." He bent his head and kissed Chelsea.

A long kiss. And then they both started making these harsh-breathing sounds like they were trying to move furniture around. Totally disgusting. And inappropriate.

"Would you like some privacy?" I asked.

Noah lifted his head. He gave me a killer grin. "Nah, man, we're just playing catch up. You know how it is."

"Actually, she doesn't," Chelsea said. "She doesn't have a boyfriend."

Okay, this was just getting ridiculous. She'd never been like this before. Bragging about something. Trying to make us feel like we weren't as important.

"Bummer," Noah said.

"Not really," I said. "I have total independence right now. I can do whatever I want without having to worry about anything. I'm completely happy."

"Me, too," he said and went back to kissing Chelsea.

I wondered why I had thought this was going to be a getting-to-know-Noah type of dinner, talking about our summer, sharing our plans. Instead it was an extension of what had happened in the front yard.

I looked at Amy. She rolled her brown eyes. Apparently, like me, she was wishing we'd stayed home to dine on peanut butter and jelly sandwiches.

The waitress arrived with our food. I'd ordered popcorn shrimp. Tiny little fried shrimp. They came in a basket with fries.

The waitress set the Admiral's Feast—every seafood imaginable spread out on two platters—in front of Noah.

"Wicked awesome," Noah said. The front legs of his chair hit the planked flooring with a resounding thud that shook the deck.

Chelsea looked startled, as though she hadn't expected him to make a move toward his food—casting her aside to do it.

"I can't believe you're going to eat all that," Amy said.

"Just watch," he said.

"I'd rather not," Amy replied. She started eating her salad.

"All men have large appetites," Chelsea said. "Especially Noah." She looked at him like he was some sort of superhero.

"So what are you doing this summer, Noah?" I asked. Trying to be pleasant. Trying to care. He was, after all, Chelsea's boyfriend. And she was one of my best friends. If he was important to her, he was important to me.

"Hanging out with Chels."

Smiling, she snuggled up against him, while he kept eating.

"What else?" I asked.

"That's pretty much it." He looked at her. "I missed you, babe."

Then he kissed her again.

"Chelsea had a lot of nerve making us split the bill three ways," Amy said, as we were walking back to the beach house.

Chelsea had insisted that because Noah had driven us to the restaurant, we should buy his dinner. The Sandpiper was a whopping one and a half miles from where we were living. How much gas had it taken?

Rather than cram ourselves back into the cab of his truck, Amy and I had decided to walk.

"I know," I said. But I'd paid up, because I didn't want to get into an argument at the restaurant.

"My salad was four bucks," Amy said. "His feast was thirty. Then his dessert and all those beers . . . we should have said no."

"Then we would have looked like jerks, because she made the suggestion with him sitting right there."

"I think Chelsea's parents gave her money for the summer. All I have is what I've saved up, plus what I make at the campground."

"We were being nice."

"We were being chicken."

I looked over at her. Her sunglasses were perched on top of her head, holding her hair back from her face.

"We just didn't want to get into a fight," she said.

I nodded, hating that the truth made us sound so weak. "I know."

"Does she seem different to you?"

"It's just—" I began.

"—that she has a boyfriend and we don't?"

I laughed. "Exactly."

We walked along in silence for a while. Or as silent as it can be when you're on an island and the sea is roaring around you. Twilight had arrived and stars were starting to pop out in the sky.

"What do you think he meant when he said he was spending the summer hanging out with Chelsea?" Amy asked.

"I guess he's going to come see her a lot."

"I'm not jealous that she has a boyfriend," Amy said.

"Me either" is what I said. Although a small part of me was a teensy bit jealous. The island could be a romantic place. Walking in the pale moonlight along the sandy beach with a guy . . .

I found myself thinking of deep blue eyes, gazing into mine, a crooked smile—

"But it's supposed to be *our* summer, right?" Amy asked, dragging me back to reality. "You, me, Chelsea."

"Right. This is supposed to be, like, a long good-bye."

"Isn't that the name of a movie?" Amy asked.

"I think so, yeah. We're shoring up memories."

"Memories of spending all my money on Chelsea's boyfriend."

"You could have said no," I told her, tired of the subject already.

"But I would have looked cheap if you didn't say no."

"No, you wouldn't have."

"Yes, I would. And then she would have been mad at me."

"But now you're mad at me for not saying no."

She shuffled along for a little while before saying, "Yeah, a little."

"I can't read your mind, Amy. I didn't know it would bother you this much."

"Doesn't it bother you?"

"It did when she first suggested it. But we paid. So now we move on."

"I guess. But next time, I'm going to say no."

"We'll both say no." And I would. I felt like Chelsea had taken advantage and put us in an awkward position. I'd be ready next time. I hoped anyway. I wanted to change the subject. "Want to stop in the video store and get a chick flick to watch tonight?"

"Definitely."

It had grown darker by the time we selected a couple of movies. We paid the rental and headed back out. We walked up the road and saw the beach house, the lights from inside spilling out into the night. It was a welcoming sight. And I was filled with contentment and peace. We'd had a few rocky moments yesterday and this evening, but that was to be expected. We'd all done countless things together, but we'd never lived together.

Amy and I went inside, climbed the stairs, and went into the living room. The TV was turned to a baseball game. Noah was sitting on the couch, his bare feet on the coffee table. Chelsea was tucked up against his side.

"Hey, y'all," I said. "We were thinking of watching a movie."

Noah looked blankly at the two DVDs I held up. "I found a baseball game," he said.

"Right," I said. I thought about calling for a vote, but no way was Chelsea going to vote with me and Amy. Then we'd be tied. And have accomplished nothing.

"Maybe we'll watch them later," I offered.

"There's a Bruce Willis movie on later," he said.

I hit the DVD cases together. They made an echoing clapping sound. "Maybe tomorrow then."

CHAPTER 8

"This is cute," Chelsea said.

She was holding a music box with a mermaid carved into the lid. Another order of souvenirs had arrived. Mrs. P had decided not to bother opening the snack bar today. So Amy was sitting on the floor with us, trying to get all the souvenirs counted and displayed.

"What's it play?" she asked.

"The theme song from *The Little Mermaid*, what else? I love music boxes. I might have to buy it."

"Chels, we're supposed to be stocking, not buying," I reminded her.

"But buying is so much more fun." With a sigh she put the box inside the glass case where we kept fragile and expensive souvenirs. "If

Noah ever asks you what he can get me, be sure to tell him I like music boxes."

"He should know you well enough that he shouldn't have to ask us," Amy said.

"Get real. Guys are totally clueless when it comes to knowing what a girl wants."

"So true," Mrs. P said. "I have a rule. Nothing that plugs in or is stored in the garage."

We laughed, Mrs. P smiled. "You think I'm kidding. But one year I got a hydraulic floor jack."

"Why?" I asked.

Mrs. P shook her head. "Haven't a clue."

"I think I'll have a serious talk with Noah," Chelsea said. "I really don't want anything like that."

"Oh, look at these," Amy said. She held up a pair of dolphin-shaped earrings. Most of our souvenir jewelry had some sort of nautical design. She looked at Mrs. P. "We get a discount on the souvenirs, too, right?"

"Right."

"I'm going to get these." Amy set them aside.

"Then I'm going to get the music box," Chelsea said.

They had no willpower. I had to admit that opening the boxes, checking to see what had come in was a lot like opening presents at Christmas. The difference was that you weren't supposed to keep what was inside. Before I could remind them about our budget, Mrs. P said, "Jennifer, did you want to take your lunch break?"

"Sure. I'll be by the pool if you need me."

I went into the office and grabbed my beach bag. These were the lazy days, before the madness that would arrive this weekend, and I intended to make the most of it. And not by buying souvenirs. As I went through the door, putting on my sunglasses, I could hear Amy and Chelsea exclaiming over another terrific find, and Mrs. P laughing. She probably should have sent them to lunch early, so we'd have souvenirs left for our customers.

I crossed over to the pool, opened the gate, and went inside. Only one of the chaise lounges looked occupied. A rumpled towel was resting on one end. I could see a body streaking beneath the water. I went to the other side of the pool and dropped onto a chaise. I took off my shoes and pulled off my CCR shirt and shorts. I was wearing my bathing suit. My belly button ring was a dolphin that curved around my navel. Seeing it reflecting in the sunlight forced me to admit that last summer I'd been as bad as Amy and Chelsea when it came to opening the boxes of souvenirs. I was beyond that this summer. I truly was. I wasn't going to look to see if we'd gotten another pair of dolphin earrings.

I gathered up my hair, twisted it, and clipped it on top of my head. I opened my bag and pulled out the old reliable X-Men-strength lotion. I'd only be out here for about fifteen minutes, but still—

"Need help putting that on?"

I shifted my gaze to the pool. Blue Eyes stood in the shallow end, water dripping from his hair, down his chest. I'd *thought* maybe he was the one gliding through the water. Okay, "thought" was too tame a word. I'd desperately *hoped*. Could I get any more pathetic?

"Your hands are wet," I said lamely.

"They dry off—I know how to use a towel."

Of course he did. I'd hoped to see him, and now I didn't know where to take that hope. I reached into my bag and pulled out my towel. "If you're sure you don't mind."

He grinned. "Are you crazy? I'm a guy. You're a girl. Why would I mind?"

He put his hands on the side of the pool and hoisted himself out of the water. Oh, my goodness. He was beautiful. Bronzed. I figured he spent a lot of his time in the sun and surf. The whole idea behind camping on the beach, I guessed.

He took the towel and sat on the edge of the chaise, slightly behind me, so he could get to my back more easily.

"I thought you'd be out exploring the island," I said.

"Late night. Zach is still asleep."

I wasn't going to ask him what he'd been doing that kept him out so late—or with whom he might have been doing it. It was truly none of my business. No matter how badly I wanted to ask.

He tossed the towel in front of me and took the bottle. I held my breath, waiting for that first touch.

"I saw you last night," he said.

My breath rushed out with his comment, then he was gliding the lotion on my back and shoulders.

"Where?" I asked.

"At the Sandpiper."

Which meant he saw the Noah and Chelsea show. I was totally embarrassed. I felt a need to explain. "Chelsea and Noah hadn't seen each other for a while."

"That would be the couple you were with."

"Right. The other girl is Amy. They're my roommates."

"You live on the island?" he asked.

I nodded. "My grandparents are lending us their beach house for the summer."

"Cool."

"It really is. I love being on the island."

"Why? It's hot. Sand gets into everything. Seagulls are forever dropping little surprises on you. The breeze blows constantly."

I twisted around and stared at him. "If you don't like the island, why are you here?"

"I do like it. I'm just wondering why you do."

How to explain?

"The attitude. One summer, I was walking by some shops in the middle of the day with my granddad. We passed a little shop that was closed. The owner had taped a handwritten sign to the door. *Closed due to lack of interest. Come back tomorrow.*

"My granddad told me the guy was on 'island time.' He says when you're on the island you should just let your moods guide you. He doesn't even wear a watch."

"Island time. I like that. Too bad I'm not on it right now." He handed my lotion back to me and stood. "I need to hit the shower before I lose my privileges."

I looked up at him, feeling disappointed and guilty. Wishing we were both on island time right now. "I'd extend them if I could."

"Don't worry about it. I understand how business works. I'll see you around."

I hope so, I thought. Of course, I didn't say it. I just flopped back on the chair, wishing I could do something. If he was here for the showers, and the showers became off limits, would he leave? And if he did, would I care?

❋ ❋ ❋

"He's going into the army at the end of the summer," I told Mr. P.

We were inside the marina where he was checking in the order of supplies he'd received. This week was all about gearing up for the summer ahead.

"I see," he murmured.

"You were in the army," I reminded him.

He looked at me. I'd finally gotten his attention.

"What do you want, Jennifer?"

I didn't really know.

"I thought maybe you could make an exception? Service to our country and all that? I don't think he can afford to pay ten dollars every day for a shower."

"How long is he staying?"

"I'm not sure."

He puckered his lips, slipped his finger beneath his cap, and scratched his head. "Okay. I can use extra help through the weekend. If he's willing to give me a couple of hours each morning on the maintenance crew, then he can use the showers, no charge. If he's interested, tell him to come talk to me."

"Okay. Thanks!"

I hurried out of the marina, a towel wrapped around my waist, and my flip-flops flapping. I didn't have much time left to take a quick shower and get back into uniform. And I still hadn't eaten the sandwich I'd packed for lunch. I rounded the corner of the main building, heading for Dylan's tent when I saw him walking from the showers.

No, he didn't walk exactly. He prowled. Long, sure strides. A loose-jointed kind of walk, like he wasn't in any hurry. That he'd get where he wanted to be when he wanted to be there.

He was in jeans, a T-shirt, and boots. His bike-riding getup, no doubt.

"Dylan!" I called and waved.

He stopped and I rushed over. He was grinning by the time I got there.

"Hey, need more lotion put on your back?" he asked.

I laughed. "No, but thanks anyway. I just wanted to tell you that I talked with the owner." I told him about Mr. P's offer.

"What would I be doing?" he asked.

I shrugged. "Whatever needs to be done. Picking up trash, cleaning the showers. Whatever."

"A couple of hours a day, huh?"

I nodded. "Yeah."

"Sounds fair enough. I'll talk to him." His lopsided grin grew and he touched my shoulder. "Thanks for looking out for me."

My heart did that trying-to-burst-through-my-chest thing. "Sure. No problem."

I watched him walk away. At least now I knew he was planning to stay through the weekend.

CHAPTER 9

"When is Noah leaving?" I asked.

It was Friday morning, the big Memorial Day weekend was upon us, and Amy and I were both a little stressed as we stood in the kitchen. We'd ended up taking the videos back last night without a chance to watch them, because Noah had taken permanent possession of the TV's remote and parked his butt on the couch all week. Chelsea was using the last of our eggs to cook him an omelet.

"Chelsea, when is Noah leaving?" I asked again, with a little more firmness in my voice.

She shrugged. "He's not."

"What do you mean he's not?" Amy asked.

"You're smart," Chelsea said. "What do you think it means?"

"He can't stay here forever," I said.

Chelsea looked at me as though I was nuts. "Chill. Of course not," she said.

For a second I felt relieved.

"He'll leave at the end of the summer, like all of us."

Then I felt like fireworks had gone off inside my head. "He can't stay here! He wasn't part of the arrangement we made with my grandparents."

A visible ripple went through her, from the top of her head to her bare feet. "I have a bedroom, I pay a third of the bills. I should be able to do whatever I want with that room. And I want to share it with Noah. He doesn't want to go anywhere without me."

"You pay a third of the bills, but Noah is a fourth person in the house."

"You know, Jen, you're going to do great majoring in business, because you have this counting thing down pat," she said snidely.

"Chelsea, he spends an hour in the shower. That's a lot of water. Which we have to pay for. He eats our food like it's free. He hogs the TV. He does no chores. He doesn't help us out at all. He contributes nothing except sand on the floor." Sand that I found myself sweeping up twice a day.

"Were you practicing that little speech all night?"

I looked to Amy for help, but all she did was nod and say, "It *was* good."

I sighed. She might not want Chelsea mad at her, but she was making *me* mad. I turned back to Chelsea. "He can't stay."

"I love him."

She gave me a defiant glare, as though those three little words were all it took to make everything all right.

"Don't you want me to be happy?" she added.

How could I argue with that? If I said I wanted her to be happy, then she'd say that she needed Noah . . . and if I said that I didn't want her to be happy, then I'd be lying.

She smiled triumphantly, picked up the plate of eggs, and walked out of the kitchen.

They were demons. Every one of them. Disguised as normal people going camping.

Their trailers were too big for the campsites;

the sites were too small for the trailers. They didn't like their neighbor. They liked another site better and wanted to move. But in the meantime that site had been rented to someone else. . . .

It was madness, mayhem, insanity.

Instead of getting off at five, Amy, Chelsea, and I ended up working until eight, even though the next shift had arrived. We were simply bombarded with too many people trying to get registered, trying to buy things in the store, wanting snacks from the snack bar.

By the time Mrs. P finally cut us loose, I was completely worn out. And still brooding over the Noah situation and my inability to come up with a response for Chelsea that would make her see things my way.

I didn't want to lose Chelsea as a friend, and I didn't know how to make her understand that Noah wasn't part of the equation when we'd made our plans for the summer.

Amy started the car and we headed out of the campground. We were on the main road, driving at a fast clip before Amy spoke. "I can't believe how tired I am. Where do all these people come from? And why are they addicted to hot dogs?"

"Rough day?" I asked.

"Like you would not believe. Even though I'm inside, I get so hot working behind the snack bar—"

"Speaking of hot," Chelsea interrupted. "Why is steam coming out from under the hood of your car?"

I unbuckled and scooted forward. Sure enough, there was a little vapor trail easing out from beneath the hood and quickly disappearing. "What's your temperature gauge show?"

"It's heading toward the red."

"Then you'd better pull over."

Amy drove off the road onto the grass and turned off the engine. All three of us groaned at once.

"This is so not good," Chelsea said. "I'll call Noah."

Was it possible that Noah's value was about to show itself? Amy and I got out of the car and walked around to the front. There was actually quite a bit of traffic whizzing by, but no one was stopping. The start of a holiday weekend, and everyone had places to go, things to do.

"What should we do?" she asked.

"I guess we should open the hood."

"Do we even know what we're looking for?"

"Probably a busted hose or something."

"Let's just wait for Noah."

Chelsea climbed out of the car. "He's not answering his phone."

Great! His one chance to be a knight in shining armor.

"So what now?" I asked.

"I guess we wave someone down," Chelsea said.

"No way!" Amy said. "Haven't you seen *Breakdown*?"

"That was fiction," I said.

"Based on fact," Amy said.

"No, it wasn't," I said.

"When did you get to be such a scaredy cat?" Chelsea asked.

"I'm cautious."

"You're chicken."

"Guys, this isn't helping. Let's just open the hood and see what we can figure out." Besides, I thought an open hood would serve as an

SOS to the passersby who had yet to realize that a car sitting on the side of the road wasn't normal.

Two motorcycles whizzed by, headed toward town, then one did a U-turn, followed by the other.

"Help might be on the way," I said.

They cut across the road and onto the grass, coming to a stop just short of the car. It sounded like thunder rumbling around us. They cut the engines, but my ears still rung with the sound. Then they removed their helmets. And I knew an instant of gladness that went far beyond the fact that these were guys and fixing cars was a guy thing.

"Looks like you got trouble," Dylan said as he strode over to me.

"Yeah."

"My boyfriend isn't answering his phone," Chelsea said.

Dylan looked at her, nodded, then turned his attention back to me. "Want us to take a look?"

"Definitely."

I made quick introductions. Zach ducked

into the car to release the latch on the hood, then Dylan lifted it. I tried not to notice the way his muscles rippled, but it was a little hard not to when his dark gray T-shirt stretched across his back. He was way buff.

"He must work out," Chelsea whispered, and there was definite appreciation in her voice.

Amy eased toward the car and stood on her toes to look under the hood—like she thought the additional distance would either give her a better view or keep her safe from any boiling water. "So?" she asked.

Dylan smiled at her, and I wished I'd eased up to look under the hood. "Busted hose. Easy enough to fix." He turned and looked up the road in the direction that they'd been going—toward Surf Town. "Zach, you want to head into town and see if you can find an auto shop?"

"Sure. Who wants to go with me?" Zach grinned, while we were all exchanging glances. "Come on. Don't be shy. I can't handle the motorcycle and hold a hose."

"I guess I'll go since it's my car," Amy said, sounding a little like she was answering a summons to ride into hell.

After Zach and Amy left on his motorcycle, Chelsea walked off, holding the phone to her ear, trying to get in touch with Noah, I guessed. Dylan took a multipurpose knife out of his pocket. He pulled out a section that could be used as a screwdriver and went to work loosening the clamps that held the busted hose in place. I leaned against the hood, watching.

"It sure was our good luck that you came by," I said.

A motor home drove past us, headed for the campground.

"Someone else would have stopped," Dylan said.

Only no one else had. I watched the way his forearm bunched up as he worked. The silence started to get uncomfortable, and I thought I should say *something*.

"So, did you talk with Mr. Plackette?"

"Sure did. Zach and I have been cleaning bathrooms at the crack of dawn," he said, not looking up from his work. He'd loosened one clamp and was reaching down to get to the one holding the other end of the hose in place.

"Oh, sorry, didn't know he'd have you at it so early," I said.

"Not a problem. He wants it done before people start getting up. Makes sense. Plus it leaves most of the day free for me and Zach to do what we want."

He grunted and twisted, which brought him a little closer to me. He'd definitely showered recently. I could smell some type of spicy scent coming off his skin.

"And you get to use the showers," I said inanely.

He turned his head, our noses almost touching. I didn't realize until that moment exactly how far I'd leaned over. *Why don't you just fall over him, Jen?*

"Thanks for hooking us up with this gig."

"No problem," I hastened to reassure him.

He pulled the hose out of the car, dropped it to the ground, straightened, leaned his hip against the grille, and crossed his arms over his chest, drawing my attention to his wide shoulders and impressive biceps.

"I couldn't believe all the people at the campground today. Where did they come from?" he asked.

I held out my hands in surrender. "All over. They are all the fortunate ones who don't have to work over the holiday."

"You're not one of those, I take it."

"No way. This is what I live for. Incredible weekends like this."

He laughed. "Yeah, I bet."

The passing vehicles suddenly seemed to get louder, and I realized it was because one of them—a motorcycle—was pulling off the road and parking beside us. Amy was sitting behind Zach, a sack nestled between them. It turned out that they'd bought not only a hose but a couple of jugs of water.

It didn't take Dylan long to attach the new hose and empty the jugs of water into the radiator. We were all set to go, which should have filled me with jubilation. Instead, I was a little sorry that our reason for having the guys around was gone.

Chelsea walked back to the car and snapped

her phone closed. "I finally got in touch with Noah. For some reason his phone wasn't getting a signal earlier."

"Doesn't matter," I said. "Everything worked out."

"So how do we get to your place?" Zach asked.

I looked at him like he'd spoken in Klingon. "Our place?"

"I offered to fix them dinner, to thank them for helping us out," Amy said.

"That's cool," I said nonchalantly. I had a crazy urge to hug Amy. *Great plan! Great plan! Wish I'd thought of it.*

"Just follow this road until it dead ends," I said. "Take a right. And follow it until you reach the end of the road. Pull into the drive. That's our house. Or follow us."

"We'll follow."

Chelsea, Amy, and I got back in the car. We were chugging down the road before Chelsea looked back over her shoulder and asked, "So, is Jen going to have a little summer romance?"

I felt myself blush. "I doubt it."

"Well, if you do, I'll be a lot more understanding about you having your boyfriend around than you are about me having mine."

"That's not fair, Chelsea." It felt good to finally release what I'd been holding in all day. It had been between us, festering.

"No, it's not, Jen. You shouldn't make me feel guilty for having a boyfriend."

"This isn't about you having a boyfriend. It's about you having your boyfriend hanging around at our place 24/7."

"Why don't you like Noah?"

I wanted to scream. Other than jabbing her with a sharp stick, I didn't know how to make her get my point. "I like him just fine, but he wasn't part of the original plan."

"Love never is. It just happens."

How was I supposed to respond to that?

"I don't want to fight about this, Jen."

"I don't either."

"Then let's not."

I thought about asking Amy what she thought, but her shoulders were slightly hunched, and she was watching the road like she expected it to disappear any minute. Confrontation wasn't her thing.

Noah wasn't a bad guy. Just an unexpected addition. Learning to live with him in the beach house would really prepare me for living in a dorm room with a stranger. I could put a positive spin on this situation, look at it in such a way that it would stop driving me crazy. Because it looked like he was here to stay, regardless of how much Amy and I wished he wasn't.

"Fine," I said. "Noah can stay."

Chelsea twisted around and looked out the window. "Know what I discovered today? Old fishermen never die. They just smell like they did."

Amy and I were still laughing when we turned up the road to the house.

CHAPTER 10

I wasn't even irritated that Noah was camped out on the sofa. I introduced him to Dylan and Zach, while Amy and Chelsea went to their rooms to change.

"Beer's in the fridge, dudes," Noah said. "Help yourselves."

"Did you go grocery shopping?" I asked hopefully, because there hadn't been any beer when we left that morning.

"Nah, just made a beer run."

Of course. Let's not overlook the important things. I tamped down my irritation and walked into the kitchen. My feet were starting to ache from being on them all day. I searched the pantry and the cupboards. Nothing much. Half a package of crackers. Two heels of bread.

I went to the refrigerator. Lots of beer. I ground my teeth together. I could make beer soup.

I heard footsteps and turned. Dylan stood there.

"I have to go to the grocery store," I said.

"You don't have to cook for us. We owe you anyway."

"No, you don't. Besides, we offered to cook."

"So do it another time. It's late. Let's go out."

Everyone agreed with Dylan's suggestion. I ran upstairs and changed into a pair of low-riding jeans and a lacy top that left my midriff and pierced belly button exposed.

We went to Joe's Surf 'n Turf. Because it was Friday, a holiday weekend, the true beginning of summer, the place was as crowded as our campground. Maybe even more so.

Wall-to-wall people. I normally wouldn't have minded, but I was seriously hungry. We'd walked there, which turned out to be wise, because we wouldn't have been able to find anyplace to park outside.

But standing just inside the doorway, I was beginning to think we'd made a mistake. It would be forever before we would be able to find a place to sit and could get our food. Rock music was blasting from speakers somewhere. The place was dark with candles flickering in hurricane lamps. Along the walls hung thick ropes and netting holding seashells and starfish. Anchors leaned in the corners.

"There's a table!" Chelsea yelled.

She headed for it, with Noah right behind her. As I started to follow, Dylan put his hand on the small of my back. It was warm against my skin.

I wondered if we were on a date. Or was he simply touching me because it was so crowded in here and he didn't want to lose sight of me?

The round table was set near a wall. Dylan sat beside me. As soon as everyone was seated, Noah planted his mouth over Chelsea's like he hadn't seen her all day. Uncomfortable—again—I shifted away from her.

Which placed me almost in Dylan's lap thanks to the cramped quarters.

He grinned. "They're pretty serious."

"Yeah."

We reached for the menus stacked in the

center of the table between the napkin holder and a tray of condiments. Our fingers touched. I froze, feeling silly and self-conscious. He grabbed a menu, opened it, and set it between us.

"Hey, I get it," Noah, suddenly unlocked from Chelsea's lips, said. "Fish in the surf, cows on the turf. Cool."

I sneaked a peek at Dylan and wondered if he was studying the prices as carefully as I was. I leaned over to Chelsea and whispered, "Noah's going to have to pay his own share tonight. We walked. We didn't use his gas."

"He doesn't have any money."

"How did he buy beer?"

She gave me a pained look like I'd taken my fork and stabbed her in the back.

"Look," I said, "We can't ask the guys to pay for him, and Amy and I aren't made of money either."

"I'll take care of Noah's share," Chelsea said.

"Okay. Thanks."

One worry over with. I felt bad that Noah was broke, and I didn't like being stingy with my money, but I really didn't think it was fair for everyone else at the table to have to pay his way. Especially when the waitress came over and he ordered a triple-decker cheeseburger with a side of shrimp.

The guys ordered beers. Amy, Chelsea, and I ordered tea. It made me feel like a kid.

Until Dylan leaned back slightly and put his arm along the back of my chair. Not on my shoulder. He wasn't even touching me, but it somehow seemed intimate.

I noticed that Amy and Zach were talking. Chelsea and Noah had returned to their favorite pastime, exchanging spit. While part of me thought it would be great to have a guy who wanted to kiss me all the time, couldn't keep his hands off me, I also wanted a guy I could talk to. I wanted something more than the physical.

But when I looked at Dylan, the physical was about all I could think about. I wondered if his kisses felt as crooked as his smile. If they'd be as warm as his eyes. As deep and penetrating as his gaze while he watched me watching him.

I leaned toward him. He leaned toward me.

"It's loud in here," I said pointlessly.

"Yeah. You like working at the campground?"

"Usually. I worked there last summer. I got to meet a lot of interesting people."

"And not so interesting, I imagine."

I laughed. "Mostly interesting."

Our food arrived. I'd ordered the shrimp, my favorite. Dylan had ordered a burger. We were sharing a basket of fries.

"So how long are you guys going to be here?" Noah asked.

"We haven't decided yet," Dylan said.

"You're just camping all summer?"

"Pretty much."

"Awesome."

"Yeah, it is."

"Camping, though. Don't you get kinda yucky?" Chelsea asked.

"Only when it doesn't rain," Zach said.

Chelsea's eyes got huge. "What?"

Zach grinned. "When it rains, we just strip down and use nature's shower. When it doesn't rain, well, then we have to pay to use the man's shower."

"You don't really strip down, do you?" Chelsea asked.

"Not where anyone can see."

Chelsea gave me a funny look. I couldn't decide if she approved or not. Wasn't certain if I did either.

"What if you get all lathered up and it stops raining?" she asked.

"He's teasing you," Dylan said. "Don't believe anything Zach says."

"So what *do* you do?" Chelsea asked.

"Chels, does it really matter?" I asked. "You're never going camping."

"I might."

"Where would you plug in your curling iron?"

"Good point." She shrugged and returned her attention to Noah.

I looked at Dylan. "Sorry about the third degree on your bathing habits."

"No big deal. You like to camp?"

"I've never been camping. I'm sorta like Chelsea. I prefer modern civilization." I held up a ketchup covered French fry to make my point.

"We have ketchup."

I grinned. "And fries?"

With his mouth, he snatched the fry from

my fingers. I just sat there, staring, watching him chew.

"No fries," he finally said.

I wasn't at all certain what had just happened, but I found myself suddenly wondering if I was getting in over my head.

It was late when we finally left the Surf 'n Turf. We all started walking along the side of the road back to the house. We'd paired off again. Chelsea and Noah, naturally. Amy and Zach. Dylan and me.

We'd only gone a few yards when Dylan took my hand. "Let's walk along the beach."

I thought about letting Amy and Chelsea know, but they were already far ahead and busy with someone else anyway.

Dylan didn't wait for me to answer. He simply pulled me along between some houses. It was shadowy and dark, the houses blocking the moonlight. We walked cautiously until we reached the invisible line where houses stopped and the true beach began.

We slipped off our shoes, rolled up our cuffs, picked up our shoes, and strolled to the water's edge. It was close to midnight, but I wasn't thinking about how tired I'd be in the morning when I woke up for work. I was just thinking that I wished tonight wouldn't have to end.

Dylan let go of my hand, reached down, picked up a shell, and threw it into the surf. It was like he suddenly needed something to do.

"Your friends are nice," he said.

"Thanks. So is Zach."

"So are you."

He looked over at me, and even though it was night, there were enough lights from the buildings, the moon, and the stars for me to see that he was studying me intently.

"You're nice, too." I felt like such a dweeb. I couldn't think of anything clever to say. And that description seemed so inadequate when applied to him.

"Glad we agree that everyone's nice," he said.

Only he was more than nice. He was sexy, and he made my heart pound every time he looked at me.

"Why camping?" I asked.

"Why not?"

"Because of the whole showering in the rain thing?"

"Hey, don't knock it unless you've tried it."

"Have you?" I asked incredulously. "I mean really showered in the rain? You said Zach was teasing."

"Don't you know that there's some truth behind all teasing?"

"So you have showered in the rain?"

"Maybe."

Mr. Mysterious started walking along the shore. I fell into step beside him. The warm water washed over our feet. There was a light breeze blowing my hair around my face. I gathered my hair, holding it in place off one shoulder.

"Why did you decide to join the army?" I asked.

"No reason in particular," he said.

But he said it in a way that made me think there was a particular reason. We simply didn't know each other well enough to share the reason—whatever it was.

"So you don't have a boyfriend?" he asked quietly.

"No."

"That's hard to believe."

"I had one for a while, but it didn't work out."

"How come?"

"I don't know. Do you have a girlfriend?"

It seemed a little late to be asking. I wondered if it would make a difference to me if he did.

"I did a couple of years ago."

"Why did you break up?"

"I don't know." The same answer I'd given him.

"You miss the guy you were dating?" he asked.

"I never think about him unless someone asks me about him."

"Same here. But I'm not looking for a girlfriend."

"I'm not looking for a boyfriend."

"That's good," he said. "It would be a real bummer for me to have a girlfriend when I'm going into the army."

I wasn't sure why he was harping on not having a girlfriend, unless he thought I was interested and wanted to make sure that I knew he didn't want anything permanent.

"Do you play pool?" he asked, abruptly changing the subject to something safe.

"Yeah." I'd gotten pretty good last summer.

"What time does that game room at the campground close?"

"They lock the doors at midnight."

He lifted his wrist, pushed a button on his watch that illuminated the face. I could see it was one with all the fancy gizmos that guys seemed to like.

"It's almost midnight now. Hardly worth going back over there," he said.

"Well, actually, I have a key."

CHAPTER 11

We returned to the house to see if anyone wanted to come with us. But they were watching a Vin Diesel movie. So we left them to it.

I hadn't really considered how we were going to get to the campground until Dylan and I were back outside, and he handed me his helmet.

"I've never ridden on a motorcycle before," I confessed.

"Guess we could walk."

I laughed. "It would take us all night."

"Bad plan. Put on the helmet."

"You should wear it," I said.

"I live on the edge."

I pulled the helmet down over my head, buckled it, and climbed onto the back of his motorcycle, right behind him. He reached around, grabbed my hands, and pulled me forward, tucking my arms around him.

"Hold on tight," he called back.

And I did. Because I was terrified that I'd fall off or we'd topple over. I nearly left my stomach behind when we turned onto the main road. The bike tilted slightly and I thought, *This is it! We're going to crash!*

I tightened my hold on Dylan, and thought I heard him laugh. The bike straightened and off we went, up the road. I tried not to close my eyes, but they kept closing anyway. I was sure we weren't breaking the posted speed limit. . . .

Except, I wasn't sure. Because it certainly felt fast. Maybe it was the roar of the engine and the rush of the wind. I wished that I didn't have the helmet between us.

I wondered if he would stay long enough to break my heart.

Where did *that* crazy thought come from? Just because I was with him tonight didn't mean we'd have anything more than this.

He began to slow down. I opened my eyes, and recognized everything around me. We were almost at CCR. My stomach dipped right along with the bike when he took the turn to the campground. I was sorry to realize that I'd soon be letting go of him.

He slowed. Regretfully, I straightened away from him.

He parked right beside the Beach Hut and cut the engine. The silence and stillness were disorienting for a second. I took off the helmet.

Dylan twisted around slightly. "So what did you think of the ride?"

"Totally awesome."

"It gets addictive. I really get claustrophobic when I ride in a car now."

"I hope you don't have to drive a tank for the Army."

"Me, too."

I slid off the bike, pulled the key out of my jeans' pocket, and started up the steps. It was eerily quiet and dark around us. Using the key, I opened the door. Once we were inside, I locked it. The light from the streetlamps set around the campground poured through the windows, softly illuminating the inside of the building, along with the overheads on some of the appliances in the snack bar and the flickering lights of the video games.

"We won't be able to turn on the main lights," I said quietly. "We'll attract too much attention, and night owls will want in. But there's still plenty of light to see once your eyes adjust."

It was very shadowy in there, but we could still see what we needed to see: mainly each other and the pool table.

I watched Dylan walk over to the case that held the cue sticks. He took down two cue sticks, handed me one, and ambled to the pool table. "Where do we get the balls?"

"You drop a quarter into the slot."

He looked over his shoulder at me. "We have to pay to play?"

I suddenly felt a little daring as I sauntered over to the table. "Well, if you were an ordinary camper you would. But since you've hooked up with the unofficial assistant manager . . ." I jingled my keys, crouched down, unlocked the coin slot, and flipped a switch. The balls tumbled out into a tray at one end of the table.

Pleased with the results, I straightened and

gave him what I hoped was an I-am-good-at-this smile. "I'll break."

Because of the shadows, I couldn't see clearly into his eyes, but I could feel him studying me. He moved to the table and started arranging the balls in the rack. "So what are we going to play for?"

His voice sounded low and secretive and left me wondering what game we were really here to play.

"The joy of winning?" I asked, my confidence suddenly sliding down to my toes.

He moved the full rack to one side, then the other, up a bit, then down, before centering it in place. "That's no fun."

Very carefully, he lifted the rack, leaving the balls in place. Although we were on opposite ends of the table, I felt his gaze home in on me.

"There has to be some element of risk to make the game interesting," he said. "Otherwise, we're just smacking balls around."

I liked smacking balls around. I'd done it a lot last summer. Still, I couldn't help wondering what I'd gotten myself into here. "What did you have in mind?"

"Home-baked chocolate chip cookies."

A bubble of laughter escaped with my relief. I was expecting him to suggest a kiss, or maybe even strip pool! Something that went with the shadows and his sultry voice.

"Hey, don't laugh. I didn't expect to miss my mom's cooking so much."

"But chocolate chip cookies?"

"My weakness."

"I thought only girls craved chocolate."

"Whatever. But if I win, you bake me some chocolate chip cookies."

"And if I win?"

"You bake me some oatmeal raisin cookies."

I laughed harder. "No way are you coming out ahead either way."

"Not totally ahead. If I win, I get something I *really* like. If I lose, I get something I sorta like."

"Not happening. If you win, I'll bake you some cookies, but if I win . . . I get an unbroken sand dollar—one that isn't bought at a tourist shop. You have to find it on the beach."

Holding his cue stick to the floor like a staff, he shifted his weight to one hip. "A sand dollar?"

"Unbroken. I've always wanted to find one on the beach. I figure with you going all the way down to Mexico, you might find one. You can mail it to me here."

"All right. You got a deal. Best out of five games. Break."

I hit the white ball so it sent the other balls scattering over the table. Two solid and one striped ball went into the pockets. "I'm solid," I said.

I walked around the table, studying how the balls were now arranged and the various angles.

"You're looking at the table like you know what you're doing," he said.

"Red ball in the side pocket," I said.

Lined up my shot. *Smack, tap, bingo!* I looked back at him. "I do know what I'm doing."

He groaned. "I really don't want to spend my summer looking for the perfect sand dollar."

"So what happened to your no risk, no fun policy? Yellow ball, corner pocket." I loved the sound of balls clicking as they came into contact with each other, even more the thud of a yellow ball dropping down into the corner pocket.

"That was when I thought winning was a sure thing."

"It is a sure thing," I said, moving so I could get a better angle on the blue ball. "*My* sure thing. Blue ball, off that end, then back into this far corner." With the tip of my cue stick, I tapped the corner I was aiming for.

"No way!"

It was a tricky shot, but I was feeling confident. As geeky as it sounds, pool is all about angles, and angles are all about math. I envisioned the ball's journey, exactly where it needed to touch the side to get the necessary angle, and how hard to get the momentum it needed to reach the far corner pocket—

"Come on already."

"No talking," I said.

"You're taking this way too seriously."

"You bet. You have no idea how badly I want a sand dollar."

"What's the big deal about a sand dollar? All the tourist shops sell them."

"Like I said. Purchased sand dollars don't count. It's gotta be a washed-up-onshore-*discovered*-sand dollar. Now be quiet."

I heard him heave a deep sigh, but I wasn't going to be distracted. Besides, I wasn't just playing for the sand dollar, but the joy of beating him. I *really* wanted to beat him. I lined up my shot and *smack!* The white ball hit the blue ball. It rolled to the end with a force and angle strong enough to bounce it back toward the corner I'd indicated. It rolled, started to slow . . . no, no, no!

"It's not going to make it," Dylan said.

"Yes, it will." I tried to send forceful vibes . . .

Didn't work. The ball stopped right at the edge of the pocket. If I just breathed on it, it would drop right in. "Not fair!"

"Yes!" Dylan jabbed a fist into the air, ambled up to the table, and bent over it. "Have to admit, Jennifer, you had me shaking in my shoes." He looked up and winked at me. "Now, babe, start lining up your ingredients, 'cause tomorrow I'm eating chocolate chip cookies."

And he proceeded to clear the balls off the table with stunning swiftness and accuracy.

CHAPTER 12

"What else do we need?" Chelsea asked.

The next day, right after work—a day marked with a lot of activity in the store and at the snack bar—we'd driven over to the mainland to do some serious grocery shopping.

I looked at our list. "Chocolate chips."

After Dylan had won the second game, I'd started to suspect he was a pool hustler or something. The third game went to me and hope had returned that he'd have to find me a sand dollar. But he'd won the fourth game without me even having the opportunity to chalk up my cue stick. Although there had been no reason to play the fifth game, we had anyway. I'd won . . . but I suspected it was a pity win, him letting me regain some of my pride.

I hadn't seen him since he'd driven me back to the beach house. Amy reported that he and Zach had stopped by the snack bar for hot dogs around noon. She'd told them to show up at seven for dinner—which didn't give us a lot of time. Especially since I had to bake cookies.

"I am so not in the mood to fix something fancy," Chelsea said as we headed to the baking aisle.

"Fancy is not in a guy's vocabulary," Amy said. "All they want is an abundance of food."

"So what are we going to cook?" Chelsea asked.

"I lost a bet with Dylan, so I have to bake some chocolate chip cookies."

"You bet with him?" Amy asked.

"Yeah." I explained about our little pool tournament.

"Too bad he didn't ask for something a little sweeter," Chelsea said when I was finished.

"Like what?"

"*Duh?* A kiss?"

I didn't want to admit that when all was said and done, I'd been disappointed that we hadn't been playing for exactly that.

"Whatever. The point is, I have to bake cookies."

"And if we're heating up the oven for cookies, then we might as well fix something else in the oven. How about meatloaf?" Amy suggested.

"Yuck!" Chelsea said.

"I can make a lot of it cheaply—and guys eat a lot. Maybe you've noticed that about Noah, Chels."

"Okay," she said with a roll of her eyes. "I'll make a fruit bowl. I saw it in a magazine. You use a hollowed-out watermelon as the bowl."

"Didn't think you wanted to get fancy," I said.

"We need something to offset the boring meatloaf."

"We'll have mashed potatoes, too," Amy said. "Because we can make a lot of those pretty cheap."

"What else?" I asked as I picked up a package of chocolate chips.

"Get the other brand," Amy said. "We have a twenty-five-cent coupon for it." She pulled the coupon out of our coupon file and waved it.

I dropped the other brand of chips into the cart.

"Do we have to use coupons?" Chelsea asked. "It makes me feel so cheap."

"They triple the amount on the coupons here. We'd be stupid not to use them," Amy said.

"Even millionaires use coupons," I added, entering the cost of the chips minus the coupon into my calculator, so I could make sure that we didn't spend more than we could afford. "I read about it in a book that explained why they have so much money."

"Oh, I'm sure Bill Gates clips coupons out of the Sunday paper," Chelsea said, clearly impatient. "Get real! It's so much effort for so little return."

"Guess we could ask Noah to pay for his share of the food."

"I was wondering when you were going to start harping on that again."

"I'm not harping; it's just a fact. I wouldn't have even brought it up if you hadn't been complaining."

"I'm not complaining. I'm just tired and want to go home. It takes *soooo* long to shop, using coupons and a calculator. Let's just split up the list, get what we need, and be done with it."

"We can't, Chels. We only have a small amount of money, and it's not going to go far. I don't want to have to start taking stuff out of the bags at the cash register."

"You know, without this bitch session, we would have been three aisles closer to being finished," Amy said, totally out of character. Aching feet could do that to you.

"Fine," Chelsea said. "I won't say another word."

Yeah, right.

When we got home, Noah actually got off the couch and helped us haul in the groceries. Once we'd put everything away, we all retreated for a quick make-over session. I changed into a pair of shorts, a V-necked T, and flip-flops. I took the rubber band out of my hair and brushed it quickly, leaving the pale blond strands to rest against my shoulders. A rapid-fire reapplication of makeup, a quick misting with Gardenia Lily scent, and I was ready to go. It was amazing how my energy level got a boost just from getting out of my uniform.

Amy had beaten me back to the kitchen. She was wearing a T-shirt that had an "I," a red heart, and a picture of a German shepherd. Not that she'd ever had a German shepherd. She just liked dogs. She'd braided her dark brown hair, weaving a ribbon through it.

With her hands, she was mixing the ingredients for the ground meat in an industrial-size bowl. Better her than me. I got out the mixer and started on the cookies.

"Where's Chelsea and Noah?" I asked.

"Take a wild guess."

I didn't know why I'd bothered to ask.

"You know, I hate to say it, but I never noticed how much Chelsea complains," Amy said.

"We're just living differently than she's used to," I said.

"You'd think she'd embrace it, though. Does she really think if she was living at home that she and Noah would be all over each other as much as they are now?"

"I'm not sure Chelsea thinks beyond the moment. You know, today my horoscope warned me that someone in my life was going to be overly sensitive and that I needed to be more considerate."

"But Chelsea's been sensitive since we got here."

"Maybe the stars just noticed."

I turned on the mixer. Its loud whining ended our conversation. By the time I had the dough ready to go on the cookie sheet, Chelsea had joined us and the volume was up on the TV. I didn't have to look in the living room to know that Noah was stretched out on the couch.

I'd peeled way too many potatoes and taken the first batch of cookies out of the oven when I heard the arrival of motorcycles. "I'll let them in."

I headed down the stairs and opened the door. Dylan and Zach were already standing there, Dylan's hand raised as though he was about to knock. I couldn't believe how glad I was to see him. He looked really good in jeans and a loose-fit Hawaiian type of shirt—a red that complemented his dark features. Zach was wearing a T-shirt that said I SEE DUMB PEOPLE.

"Hi," I said unnecessarily. "Come on in."

They stepped inside, and I closed the door.

"Something smells terrific," Dylan said.

I smiled. "I just took the first batch of cookies out of the oven. I'll even let you have one and take a chance on ruining your appetite for dinner."

He actually ate half a dozen cookies, but his appetite definitely didn't get ruined.

Believe it or not, the house didn't have a large dining table. Just the island and the small booth in the kitchen—which six of us couldn't squeeze into. When we had family gatherings, my granddad usually grilled outside and people ate on the lawn.

So we set the food on the counters. Everyone filled their plates, and we sat around the living room, eating. I was on the floor, my back against the bookcase, wondering if I should suggest a game of Monopoly when we were finished eating. Or would that be totally geeky? Totally geeky.

But I didn't want Dylan leaving as soon as he was finished eating. What could I suggest that wouldn't take the last of my savings?

"We should go to a movie tonight," Noah suddenly announced.

No way! It was after eight, long past the time when we could get in at a discounted price. I looked at Amy, not even bothering with Chelsea, because I knew she wouldn't explain that we couldn't afford it. Amy was sitting cross-legged by the Ping-Pong table. She just lowered her gaze to her plate, though, once again leaving me to be the bad guy—the one who ruined everyone's fun.

"How about tomorrow, Noah? When we can go to a matinee and the tickets are half price?"

"There is no matinee. You wouldn't be able to see the screen during the day anyway."

"What are you talking about?"

"Yesterday when I went to the mainland for my beer run, I discovered a drive-in movie theater. It's not that far from the bridge. You just pay a buck to park the vehicle. No matter how many people are inside it. Pretty cool, huh?"

"I didn't know drive-ins still existed," Dylan said.

"This one looks like a good strong wind will

blow it down, but hey, can't beat the price. Figure we throw some blankets in the bed of my truck, park it backwards, and we're all set."

"Noah, you're a genius," Chelsea said.

Her comment surprised me. I couldn't see Chelsea getting excited about watching a movie without the comfort of air-conditioning and a cushioned seat. Maybe she was just impressed that he'd come up with a suggestion that didn't involve his stomach or their lips.

"Hey, I'll even pay the buck," Noah said.

How could I not say yes to a deal like that?

CHAPTER 13

I'd never been to a drive-in before. The designated parking areas were marked with speakers. Noah backed between two of them. The speakers could actually be hung inside the windows of a car, but since we didn't have windows in the bed of the truck, Noah set them on the sides so we could hear the movie.

Watching a movie at a drive-in is one of those things that sounds better in theory. Even with all the blankets piled beneath us, it was difficult to get comfortable. Until the guys decided the best arrangement would be if they pressed their backs against the cab of the truck, and Amy, Chelsea, and I pressed our backs against them.

It felt great to be snuggled up against Dylan,

which as far as I was concerned was the best part of the drive-in experience.

I'd been surprised by the long line of vehicles coming in when we got there. Although judging by the cars with their windows fogged up, I didn't think most of these people were really here to watch the movie.

I wasn't too interested either. It wasn't exactly a blockbuster. There was a psycho on the loose and the people in the house were trying to decide who should go for help. Bad idea.

"Haven't they seen *Scream*?" I asked. "Don't they know there are rules, and you aren't supposed to go out at night or be alone or—"

"Shh!" Noah and Chelsea said at once.

Were they seriously watching this thing?

"Excuse *me,*" I whispered.

Dylan chuckled quietly. He was resting his chin on my shoulder.

"We should have brought the cookies," he said in a low voice.

"I'll let you take the leftovers back to your tent."

A girl in the movie was creeping through the

house, carrying a bat, calling for her boyfriend—who was probably already dead.

"Why are people in scary movies always so stupid?" I asked quietly. "You know the creepy guy is going to jump out—"

He did. But even though I knew it was going to happen, I screamed and jumped anyway. So did Amy and Chelsea. A total reflex. The guys laughed like it was the funniest thing. I felt like a idiot. Dylan wrapped his arms around my middle and pulled me closer against him. Perhaps the true reason Hollywood made scary movies. So guys could have an excuse for holding a girl close.

"I'll protect you," he said, and I could hear him fighting to rein in his laughter.

"I'm not scared," I shot back.

"My bad. I mistook your silence for a scream."

I twisted around and lightly slapped his shoulder. "Jerk."

I didn't mean it, of course. I was actually having fun. Even if the movie did give me chills. Or maybe it was Dylan being so close, because the chills were kind of pleasant.

"Your hair is tickling my nose," he said. "Can I move it?"

"Oh, sure."

He didn't move it aside with the carelessness I would have. He looped it behind my ear first, his finger trailing down my face around my ear. Then he roped it around to the other side.

Now I had incredibly pleasant chills, because his warm breath was skimming along my neck.

"You smell really good," he murmured.

"Gardenia Lily," I said.

"No, chocolate chip."

It was hard to laugh without making a sound, but I managed, my shoulders quaking. This guy had a one-track mind. I'd eaten some cookies before we left the house. So maybe that was why I smelled like them. Or maybe my hair had absorbed the aroma while they were baking. Or maybe he was just flirting, and I didn't really smell like anything.

He, on the other hand, smelled really spicy, so I knew he'd showered again before he came over. I wondered how long his arrangement with Mr. P would last. Had Dylan given him a definite number of days—or was he still taking it day by day? How long was he going to stay? When would he leave?

Because I was really starting to like him. And that really *was* scary.

CHAPTER 14

The movie was over a little after midnight, and we went straight back to the house. Some of us had to work the next day, after all. Zach decided to call it a night, got on his motorcycle, and headed to the campground. Dylan came inside to get the remaining cookies. Amy went to her room. Noah and Chelsea were on the couch, doing their thing.

My grandma never threw anything away. A big drawer in the kitchen was filled with empty plastic butter tubs. I pulled one out and put the cookies in it. I snapped the lid into place and held it out to Dylan. I thought he'd snatch it up and leave.

Instead he asked, "How do you get to that crow's nest up there?"

"There's stairs."

"I bet it's an awesome view."

"It is. You can see the whole island."

He waited, his eyes on mine . . . until I finally realized that he was waiting for an invitation. "Would you like to see it?"

"Yeah."

"Come on."

I set the tub on the counter and led him up the stairs to the next floor. "Amy and I sleep in the bedrooms up here," I said when we reached the landing, not certain why I felt this uncontrollable need to serve as a tour guide. I took him to the end of the hallway and opened a door that revealed the stairs that led to the crow's nest.

They were steep and narrow. I went first. At the top, I unlatched the trapdoor and pushed it up. Then I climbed out. Dylan followed and closed the door behind him.

We moved to the edge of the crow's nest. All the way around, the wall was about waist high. From there to the roof, it was open. The breeze blew around us.

"I love it up here," I confessed. "Sometimes

I come up here when I can't sleep."

"This is great," he said.

The moonlight glinted off the water of the bay. A foghorn sounded. A sheet of lightning illuminated the sky.

"A storm's coming in," I said unnecessarily.

"I can smell the rain in the air," he said.

"I guess if you didn't have the arrangement with Mr. P, you'd be showering in the rain soon."

"Might do it anyway. Want to join me?"

My mouth dropped open. I didn't know what to say.

"Just think about it," he said finally.

No problem there. Couldn't *stop* thinking about it, actually.

We were quiet, simply listening to the water lapping at the shore, the occasional rumble of thunder, growing nearer.

"It's cool that you have a guy living with you," he said after a while.

Here I was hoping his thoughts had turned to me—and he wanted to talk about Noah. I couldn't seem to escape the guy.

"Noah isn't living with me. He's living with

Chelsea. Totally, exclusively."

"But it's good that he's around. He can take care of things for you."

"Right. About the only thing he takes care of is changing the channels and buying the beer."

"You don't like having him around?"

"It's just that he wasn't expected. Chelsea invited him to move in without asking us."

"You don't like the unexpected."

"Not particularly."

"So if I want to kiss you then I should tell you first?"

Okay. This was so not where I thought we were going with this conversation, but I could live with it. I could definitely live with it.

"Not necessarily. I mean, some things, even though they're unexpected, you still anticipate them."

I felt like I was talking in circles. Nervous, anxious, excited. "I guess what I mean is that you wouldn't have to announce it, if you wanted to kiss me. You could just kiss me, and I wouldn't be upset that it came without an announcement, because—"

"Jennifer?"

"Yeah?"

"I'm going to kiss you."

Simple. Quietly spoken. And then his lips were on mine.

And his kiss wasn't at all like his smile. It wasn't crooked or one-sided. It was quite simply . . . perfect.

CHAPTER 15

The next morning I woke up to the patter of rain hitting the roof and its scent wafting in through the open window. I reached down and brought the covers that I'd kicked off during the night up to my chin to ward off the chill of the cool breeze ruffling the curtains. I snuggled down against the mattress, listening to the rain, ocean, and wind. Heavenly.

I thought of Dylan and how all this might sound to him, zipped up inside his tent. Had he stripped down and taken a shower in the rain before going inside?

I thought about his kiss. I wondered what it had meant to him, if anything. And wished it hadn't meant so much to me.

I wanted to be cool, carefree. A real island

girl who just let life happen.

But the truth was that I didn't give kisses away lightly. And I'd only once given my heart. It had hurt. And I didn't want to feel that hurt again.

Chelsea kept saying that I didn't know what it was to have a boyfriend. But I did. I knew what it was to plan my life around him, only to learn that he'd planned nothing around me.

I wanted a guy around. But I didn't want to care about him the way I was already starting to care about Dylan. Dylan who had announced that he wasn't looking for a girlfriend, Dylan who had announced that he was going to kiss me. And then had. Long, slow, without hurry.

With a moan, I clamped my pillow over my head. To block out the rain and the surf and the breeze. To stop the memories of his kiss from making my lips tingle.

To stop myself from wondering if he'd kiss me again. Tonight. After work.

After work!

I shot straight up to a sitting position. Work! Rain! *No, no, no!*

I scrambled out of bed and hurried to the

window. I looked out at the drenched, dreary world. No sun. Just a steady downpour.

In my cotton boxers and tank, I shuffled out of my bedroom and across the hallway. I knocked on Amy's door.

"Just a sec!" she called out.

I heard a thud like something dropping to the floor. A grunt. A whine?

"Amy, are you okay?"

"I'm fine! I'll be there in a sec."

I heard another thud. Then she opened the door a crack and peered out like she'd forgotten that I knew what she looked like in her underwear.

"Are you sure you're okay?" I asked.

"I'm fine. What do you need?"

"It's raining."

She pointed to her eyes and then her ears. "These work, you know."

"Do you know what people who camp on the beach do when it rains?"

She bumped into the door, a look of panic in her eyes, then closed the door, and opened it back up—but the crack was even narrower than before. I heard scratching and definite whining. No doubts now.

"What is going on in there?" I demanded to know.

"Nothing."

I pointed to my eyes and ears and repeated what she'd just told me. "These work, you know!"

"It's my room, my business."

The scratching got more frantic. She looked down, did something with her foot behind the door.

"Amy—"

"No, wait. Stop! Don't do that! No!"

She was gone, leaving the door ajar. Maybe it *was* her room, but it was *my* grandparents' house and I had a responsibility to them. I pushed on the door—

And was attacked!

The biggest rat I'd ever seen was running around my feet, jumping on my legs. I could see Amy on her knees on the floor, wiping at what looked like spilled lemonade. I didn't want to think that it wasn't exactly that.

The rat—which I realized was a dog—was yipping. I heard pounding on the stairs. Chelsea appeared. She screamed really loudly. Again. And again.

"A rat! Noah, help!"

"It's not a rat," Amy said with disgust, as she came over and picked it up. "It's a hairless Chihuahua."

It was a frisky thing, squirming in her hands.

"Where did it come from?" I asked.

Before she could answer, I heard louder pounding on the stairs. Noah appeared, a lamp in his hand held up a like a saber. Great! What did he think he was going to do with that?

"Where is it?" he asked.

Then I realized he was coming to our rescue. Chelsea put Noah between herself and us as though she didn't quite believe Amy's claim about the dog. I started laughing. This was just too much. The rain, the dog, the mess in Amy's room, Noah . . . and how much I was starting to like Dylan when I shouldn't—not this much anyway. Was he the important relationship that was going to go in a direction I didn't want, which my horoscope had forewarned me about?

That thought made me stop laughing.

"Hey, where did you get the mutt?" Noah asked, as he came the rest of the way up the stairs.

This time, with no loud noises to distract Amy, she said, "I heard him whining outside when it started raining."

"Who does he belong to?" Noah asked.

"Me, I guess."

"No, not you. He has to belong to someone else," I pointed out.

"He has no tags, not even a collar," Amy said. "I've heard about people dumping their unwanted dogs on the island."

"Well, regardless of how he got here, you can't keep him," I told her.

"Why not?"

"Who's going to take care of him while you're working?"

"I will," Noah said, as he patted the dog's head.

"Ew! No!" Chelsea said. "He looks like a rat."

"But he's not, he's a dog," Noah said. "What's his name?"

"Like I said, no tags. So I don't know," Amy said.

"He's a little thing," Noah said. "That's what I think we should call him. Tiny."

Amy grinned up at Noah like he'd finally started paying for his share of the food.

"We can't keep him. He peed on the floor," I pointed out.

"I can train him," Amy said.

I looked at Noah. "You don't even pick up your clothes. You're going to pick up after the dog?"

"Sure." He took the dog from Amy's hand. "Come on, Tiny. Let's go back to bed."

"You can't have him in my grandparents' bed!"

"I'm not. I'm going to have him in Chelsea's bed."

"But Chelsea's bed is my—" Before I could finish explaining the true ownership of the bed, Noah had disappeared down the stairs, Chelsea trotting after him.

I shook my head. "I don't believe this."

"Actually, I think he's house-trained," Amy said. "I just didn't know that he needed to go out. Now I know."

"Amy, a dog is such a hassle."

"But they love unconditionally."

I wagged my finger at her. "If he ruins anything—"

"He won't. And I'll pay for his dog food, so it won't be part of our grocery split."

I couldn't believe I was going to agree to this. "Okay."

"You came over to tell me something."

That seemed like hours ago. But the rain was still falling. "Yeah, I was asking if you knew what campers did when it rained."

"Is this like a knock-knock joke?"

"I wish. When it rains, they can't go play outside. So they play at the arcade."

"Oh."

"Yeah."

CHAPTER 16

"Do you know karate? Because your body sure is kickin'."

In my CCR uniform? Give me a break. Still, I turned to the shirtless wonder at the counter who I judged to be fairly close to my age. I smiled and said, "You come on as strong as a garlic milkshake."

He grinned. "Ah, come on. Play along. I've got no sun, no fun. Flirting with a babe is about all that's left to me."

He was kinda cute, blond hair, eyes as green as mine. He looked like he was dressed so that as soon as the rain stopped, he could be on the beach. Swim trunks, flip-flops.

"Sorry. What can I get you?" I asked.

"Are you an option?"

I laughed at his pathetic attempts to make a favorable impression on me. "No, I'm not on the menu. Your choices are limited to popcorn, nachos, or hot dogs."

"Hot dog."

"One hot dog coming up." The problem with my job in registration was that once the campground was full, I became a wandering employee. I had nothing to do so I took up the slack in the areas where others were really busy. Today the busiest place was the Beach Hut, so I found myself in the trenches with Amy.

I handed him the hot dog. "That'll be a dollar."

He paid me.

"I'm Matt by the way."

"Jennifer."

"You want to hang out tonight after you get off from work?"

"Actually, I sorta already have plans." I didn't, but I didn't want to crush him completely. He wasn't a total jerk.

"Well, if you change your mind, I met some people who are going to have a party down on the beach. Just look for the fire and the fun."

"Thanks. I'll keep it in mind."

"Excuse me, but if you have time to work here—in between flirting and getting directions to parties—there's a fly in my nachos," Mr. Warner said.

"Enjoy it!" I said to Mr. Warner. "It's on the house."

He'd come to the counter less than ten minutes before complaining that his hot dog had been undercooked. No way, but the customer is always right. Besides, how could I determine exactly how it was cooked when the whole thing was already in his stomach? So I'd given him the nachos to make him happy. Didn't charge him a cent.

I was beginning to think he wouldn't know happy if it bit him on the butt.

He put the nachos on the counter. "Dead fly. Health violation."

Okay. There *was* a dead fly, and it was gross. I took the nachos and dumped them in the trash. Then I turned back to him. "Popcorn?"

He nodded.

I scooped the popcorn into the sack and

handed it to him. "At least today you've got your shade."

"It's raining." He said it like it was my fault, like I'd done something to make it rain. Oh, to have such power. I'd turn him into a toad.

"Exactly, so there's no sun, which is what you were complaining about the other day."

"I like the sun."

"I thought you wanted shade."

"You have to have sun to have shade."

Okay. This was going nowhere. "Enjoy the popcorn."

Fifteen hot dogs, six nachos, and eight bags of popcorn later, I was beginning to wonder if people would ever stop eating. Or if it would ever stop raining.

"Can you believe how busy it is in here?" Amy asked. "My feet are killing me."

"Do you want to take a break?"

"Where would I go? It's raining outside."

"To the store? Get a candy bar or something? Visit with Chelsea?"

A covered walkway joined the snack bar to the main building and store.

"Nah, she's probably busy, too. Are Dylan and Zach coming to the house tonight?"

"I don't know. Is it okay if they do? I mean, you seemed to get along with Zach."

"Yeah, he's nice. But you know they're leaving in a few days."

"I know."

Amy nodded. "You just seemed to really have an interest in Dylan."

"I like him . . . a lot," I reluctantly admitted.

"Don't get hurt."

"I won't. I mean, I know we can't have anything serious. It's just fun to hang around with him."

"Hey, a guy told me about a party tonight, on the beach."

"Yeah, I heard the same rumor."

"Maybe we should think about going. You know, if it ever stops raining."

I almost said that I'd have to check with Dylan. That made me sound so much like Chelsea, and I really didn't want to do that. Dylan wasn't my boyfriend. I didn't know for sure if I'd see him after work.

"Let's think about it," I said instead.

"Okay."

I heard a giggle followed by a familiar laugh. I looked toward the game room and saw Dylan playing pool with some girl in cutoffs and a halter top. I hadn't seen him come in, and I wished that I hadn't seen him now.

"It's raining," Amy said, like she could read my mind. "He has to do something."

"I know." But I couldn't take my eyes off him. The familiar way he lined up the shot. The way he focused all his attention on the ball and not the girl—thank goodness. He sent the ball straight into the pocket. He grinned at the girl like he'd won something. I didn't want to think about what they might have been wagering.

"I'd better make some more popcorn," I said.

Amy followed along behind me like the little dog she'd had in her room that morning.

"It doesn't mean anything."

"What?" I asked curtly.

"That he's playing with her."

"He kissed me last night, Amy."

"Oh. Wow. Geez."

I poured popcorn kernels into the pan.

"You got serious fast," she said.

I lifted a shoulder. "It was just a kiss. It didn't mean anything."

"It did to me."

I swung around. Dylan was standing there, folded over, arms resting on the counter. His eyes were twinkling. Was he always in a good mood?

I couldn't stop myself. I asked, "Who won the game?"

"I saw you watching."

"It was kinda hard to miss."

"I wasn't playing with Susan—"

"Susan?" I interrupted, hating this little green-eyed monster sitting on my shoulder.

"The girl you saw talking to me. She was telling me about a party she and her boyfriend are having on the beach tonight—if it stops raining."

"Her boyfriend?" Okay, I was starting to sound like an irritating echo, but I seemed unable to stop myself from repeating everything. Or being relieved. He hadn't been flirting. He'd just been talking. And she had a boyfriend!

He gave me his familiar crooked grin. "Yeah. Tom. Anyway, they're inviting people. I was wondering if you wanted to go."

Guilt hit me, because I'd gotten jealous when I had absolutely no right to. "You know, you don't have to hang out with me. I mean, summer's short, and you need to make the most of your time—"

"Hanging out with you *is* making the most of my time. But if you're not interested—"

"No, I am." I just hadn't expected to meet someone I wanted to spend time with, someone who would be leaving in a few days. Someone who was hot and cool at the same time. Who made my heart swell. Who gave me crooked smiles and slow kisses.

"Great. Let the gang know." His grin broadened. "What time do you get off?"

"Around four."

"Okay. We'll meet you at your place."

He turned to go, then stopped and looked back at me. "You weren't jealous were you? About Susan, I mean."

"Of course not."

He winked at me. "Too bad."

Now what in the world did he mean by that?

CHAPTER 17

The rain stopped and the sun came out just a little after one. Everyone evacuated the campground like we'd announced that seashells were turning into money. Chelsea and I were in the cooler, restocking the almost empty metal shelves—people had been in the store buying things like crazy all morning.

"Zach was in here earlier," she said, stopping for a minute to rub her nose with a gloved hand. "He said we're all going to a party tonight."

"On the beach."

"Sounds like fun."

"I think it will be."

"Noah really likes Zach and Dylan. I think he's going to hang out with them today."

"Doing what?"

"I don't know. Exploring the island. Playing in the surf." She sighed. "I so do not want to be here."

"We'll get out of the cooler faster if we keep working," I said, as I continued to put cans on the shelves.

"I'm not talking about the cooler. I'm talking about working, period. It's a total bummer, completely lame when everyone else can play and we have to work."

"If we don't work, we don't get paid, and if we don't get paid, how can we afford to live in the beach house?"

"I don't know." She started stacking cans on the shelves again. "It just seems so unfair. I mean, it's summer! We should be out soaking up the rays, lying on the sand, playing in the surf, not being a slave to the dollar."

Not being a slave to the dollar? A bit melodramatic. Besides, did she truly not get that without income, we had absolutely nothing? It wasn't as if Noah was chipping in anything toward our expenses.

It was like she was seeking some sort of Utopia that didn't exist. She wanted a world of her and Noah. No work, no cleaning, no cooking, no responsibilities. I was getting tired of arguing with her.

"So quit," I said, half-jokingly.

"I think I'm going to."

I stared at her. "You can't quit."

"Why not? It's a free country."

"Mrs. P hired you because I promised her you were dependable. Besides, it'll leave us short an employee, and you can see how busy we are."

"I *hate* it, Jen. Hate, hate, hate it. I hate the fishermen who smell like they're storing bait in their pockets. I hate the girls who come in here wearing their bathing suits, smelling like coconut oil, reminding me that they're in the sun while I'm under fluorescent lights. I hate the guys who remind me how much I miss Noah. I hate freezing my butt off, stocking the cooler, knowing that in an hour I'm going to have to stock it again. I absolutely hate every second of every minute that I'm here!"

Then she sat down on a case of root beer, buried her face in her hands, and burst into tears.

I couldn't believe this. One of the cooler doors opened, warm air rushed in, a hand grabbed a drink, the door closed. Okay. So all the campers hadn't left, or maybe a fisherman had come in. Not that it mattered. I stared at Chelsea. Her shoulders were bouncing up and down. She didn't seem to have noticed that someone had come in and taken a drink.

I knelt in front of her. "Chels, don't cry. Your tears will freeze."

"It's not that cold in here."

"You just said your butt was freezing."

She looked up, sniffed, rubbed her nose. "I miss Noah."

"You'll see him in a couple of hours."

"I don't like not being with him. He's alone all day. And I'm alone here."

"How can you feel alone with two hundred campers around?"

"I can't explain it. And I know you can't understand—"

"Because I don't have a boyfriend," I finished for her.

She nodded. "I'm afraid that if I'm not with him, he'll stop loving me."

I felt like she'd punched me. She was my best friend. I didn't want to see her hurting, didn't want her to have doubts about herself.

"Oh, Chels. He's not going to stop loving you. And you can't be with him *all* the time." And it occurred to me that if she was, *then* he might stop loving her, because she might get on his nerves as much as she was getting on mine. I was beginning to think that Chelsea was best taken in small doses.

"What if he goes out on the beach and meets someone he likes better?"

"He won't."

"How do you know?"

"Because you're so wonderful. How could he possibly meet anyone he liked better than you?"

"You're just saying that because you're my best friend."

"No, I'm not. I'm saying it so you'll stop crying and we can get out of the cooler. More than that I'm saying it because now *my* butt is freezing."

She laughed.

"Noah isn't going to find anyone better, Chels,

because there isn't anyone better. I mean that."

She hugged me. "I'm being silly, I know I am. Let's finish up so we can get out of here."

Abruptly she stood and went back to work.

Chelsea, Amy, and I had always shared our fears and doubts. But this was something different, and I wasn't exactly sure what was going on. Noah seemed to be crazy in love with Chelsea. Why was she worried?

CHAPTER 18

By the time we got to the house, Dylan and Zach were already there, in the living room, drinking beer, watching one of the *Sopranos* DVDs with Noah. Chelsea plopped down on the couch beside him. He swung his arm around her, drew her up close, and started kissing her like they'd never stopped.

Yeah, right, Chels. He's going to find someone he likes better.

"Sorry we're late," I announced.

Dylan stood. It always made my heart thud when I saw all of him. He was so in shape. He grinned.

"We have a surprise for you."

I followed him into the kitchen. Holding

Tiny, Amy was standing beside a large bucket, looking inside.

"There are crabs in here," she said.

"Yeah, Zach and I caught them this afternoon. We were hoping for fish, but they weren't biting. Lots of crabs, though, stealing the bait off our hooks, so we decided that we'd show them."

I glanced in the bucket. The crabs were huge, with blue backs and giant claws. I couldn't see exactly how many there were because they were piled on top of each other, making little hissing noises.

"Do you know how to cook them?" Dylan asked.

"Sure," I said, smiling. "Just boil some water, season it, and toss them in."

"But they're alive," Amy said.

"Well, yeah, that's how you have to cook them. Like lobsters."

"It seems mean."

"They're crabs, Amy."

She held up a hand and began to back away. "I don't want to have anything to do with cooking something that's alive."

"Fine, I'll do it." Alone, since Chelsea was still busy on the couch.

"I'm not going to eat them," Amy said. "I'm sorry. I just can't. I've looked into their eyes."

"You can barely see their eyes."

"We connected."

I couldn't believe this. "Fine, fine, fine."

I opened a lower cabinet and pulled out the large pot that I'd seen my grandma use to cook the crabs that Granddad caught. It clanked when I dropped it into the sink. I turned on the water.

"I'm going to go take a shower. I smell like hot dogs," Amy said. "I'll fix a salad when I'm done."

"Okay."

I turned off the water, went to grab the pot handles, and found other hands there, arms that had reached across in front of me. I went completely still, barely breathing. Dylan was so close that I could smell the cologne he was wearing, something spicy and rich.

"I'll get it," he said.

I looked up into his eyes, and my heart

started hammering. "It was really sweet of you and Zach to catch us some supper."

"We drank your beer and used your shower. Noah said it was okay, since we were already over here, dropping off the crabs. The using-the-shower part."

He'd been in my shower? That seemed so intimate.

"Yeah, that's cool. Not a problem."

I stepped back, and he lifted the pot out of the sink. The muscles in his forearms flexed. It was a huge pot and with all the water I'd put in it, it was heavy. I'm not sure why I'd thought I could lift and carry it to the stove.

We were the only two in the kitchen now. Suddenly I felt self-conscious. I rubbed my hands on my shorts. "I think I saw some crab boil in the pantry." Another inane thing to say—I was on quite a roll.

I opened the pantry door and looked inside. Yep, crab boil all right. About a dozen boxes. Gran must have gotten them on sale.

They say that a watched pot never boils, and ours was certainly being watched. After I put the packet of crab boil in, Dylan and I stood guard over the pot like we expected it to try to escape. I could hear the crabs moving around in the bucket. They probably did want to escape.

It wouldn't be dark for a couple of hours. Then I figured we'd go find that party on the beach.

"Is it okay that we're here?" Dylan asked.

I snapped my head around and looked at him. "Yeah, sure."

"What's bothering you?"

I shook my head. "I don't know."

He studied me. "Is it because I kissed you last night?"

"A little . . . I think. You're just passing through. I mean, you're going to meet lots of girls on lots of beaches . . . And I have no right to even care, and I don't know why I do . . . and you were in my shower . . . and I'm rambling like an idiot."

He cocked his head to the side. "So you want me to leave?"

"No. God, no." I so didn't want that. But I didn't know what I did want. I was afraid that I wanted what I couldn't have. And that was insane because I'd known this guy for only a few days. But it seemed so much longer. Like forever. The way I'd felt when I first met Chelsea and Amy—that in an instant we were part of something special.

"Look, maybe I better clear things up," he said. "The army isn't prison, but it's not a summer spent on the beach either. I just want to have a good time while I can. And while I'm on this island, I'd like that good time to be with you. But no strings. Nothing permanent. If you're cool with that—"

"I am," I said hastily. I didn't want to know what the alternative was if I wasn't cool with it. Because I did like him. I liked him a lot. So I forced myself to say, "Besides, when you leave, other guys will come along. And I'll move on."

He furrowed his brow. "Yeah, that's what you should do . . . move on to other guys."

"Because you're so right. This is summer, we're both going places at the end of it, and we need to make the most of these months, have fun, meet people."

"Exactly."

"So you're my now guy."

"I just want to be clear on where I'm coming from and why, because if this wasn't my last chance—"

Whatever he was going to say went unsaid as a sizzling sound made us both jump to attention. We'd been watching each other instead of the pot, and the water had boiled over. I lowered the flame, and the water settled into a rolling simmer.

I looked over at him, wondering if he was going to finish whatever it was he was about to say, but he was staring at the pot like it contained answers.

"You okay?" I asked.

He glanced over at me and grinned. "Yeah. Let's get these crabs cooked. Any idea how we go about it without getting pinched?"

"We have some long tongs, or you could try dumping them in."

"Dumping sounds like it'll work."

"And is more manly?"

"You bet."

He picked up the bucket holding the crabs. I could hear their claws and legs scratching against the metal. It seemed like their hissing got louder. I knew there was no way that they could know what awaited them. Still, I felt a little guilty, found myself wishing that Amy hadn't connected with them.

Dylan held the bucket over the pot. He angled it down. The crabs started to slide out. The first crab hit the water with a splash. The others quickly followed. Except for one. I don't know how, but suddenly it was jumping free, scrambling away.

"Shit!" Dylan yelled as it hit the edge of the stove, claws snapping, then dropped to the floor.

I screeched and hurried out of the way, as it skittered across the tile.

"Hey, what's going on?" Chelsea yelled.

"Nothing! We've got it under control!" Or at least I thought we would in time.

I was reminded of a scene out of *The Little Mermaid*. I expected to see Dylan brandishing a huge knife.

Instead he was looking around frantically, still holding the bucket. "You got a broom?"

"Yeah," I answered, unable to figure out why he wanted to clean the kitchen now.

"I'll hold the bucket, you sweep him in."

"Sweep a crab?"

"Better than trying to pick it up with our hands or a pair of tongs, 'cuz I don't think it's going to be real cooperative."

He had a point. I walked to the pantry, heard the scratching of hard legs over the floor, turned, saw the crab backing toward a corner. *Don't look in his eyes,* I told myself. *Don't let him do to you what he did to Amy.*

I opened the pantry door and grabbed the broom.

"Okay, how do we do this?" I asked.

"I'll hold the bucket on the floor, like a dust-pan, you sweep him in."

Right. Sounded simple enough.

But the crab was having nothing to do with our brilliant plan. He skittered one way and when I went after him, he skittered the other. Then he grabbed the edge of the broom. Gosh, he had huge claws. They looked like they could do some real damage.

"Your mistake, buddy," I said through grit-ted teeth.

Dylan was crouched down, holding the

bucket in place on the floor. I pushed the crab into the bucket, but when I brought the broom out, he came back out right along with it. I put the broom and him back into the bucket, then banged the crab again the side. But the tenacious creature held on tight.

"He won't let go!"

"Try carrying him to the pot."

"I don't think I can do that."

"Why not? He's holding on tight enough."

"I mean it seems . . . cruel. To carry him to his death."

"He's a crab, Jennifer."

Okay. Hadn't I said the same thing to Amy? "I know, but—"

Dylan stood up and took the broom. He lifted it and the crab, carrying them both to the stove. As he started lowering the crab into the pot, I almost shouted at the silly thing to let go.

"He fought the brave fight. Maybe we should give him his freedom," I announced—but too late.

The crab was in the water. And suddenly I wasn't hungry anymore.

CHAPTER 19

Hunger returned with a vengeance, though. We sat on the balcony, cracking crab claws and eating the meat with melted butter and cocktail sauce. The sun was going down by the time we finished and set off to find the beach party.

Because we figured beer would be readily available in abundance and because the muggy heat of the day had given way to sultry island breezes, we decided to walk. We did our usual pairing up. On the way home from work, Amy had stopped at a store and picked up a collar and leash for Tiny. He was trotting along beside her.

"Where did she find the dog?" Dylan asked.

"I don't know. She heard him last night. She's like that. Taking in the strays."

Noah and Chelsea were up ahead, wound

around each other like they couldn't walk without the support of the other. I wished I had the nerve to wrap my arm around Dylan's waist, snuggled up against his side. I wished he'd swing his arm around my shoulders and pull me close.

He took my hand, and for the moment, that was good enough. We held gazes, like we thought nothing would appear in our path to trip us up. Considering all the debris that the ocean washed onto shore, it wasn't a smart move. But before we did stumble, Zach yelled, "Hey, guys! I think this is it!"

As much as I didn't want to stop looking at Dylan, I did. I could see a fire on the beach. It wasn't much of a fire. I suspected that the party planners had trouble finding dry driftwood. Even though the temperatures had risen into the high 90s that afternoon, a lot of the area hadn't dried out completely. A small crowd milled around. People who would soon be shadows as the sun sank lower.

The nice thing about summer was that night didn't fall until late, which gave us plenty of time to play. Too much time when we had to get up early to get to work.

But I wasn't thinking about work now. I was thinking about the party and being with Dylan.

We met Susan and Tom.

"So what did you guys bring?" Tom asked.

I was majorly embarrassed to have arrived empty-handed. Well, not exactly empty-handed, if I counted Dylan's hand in mine.

"We brought ourselves," Noah said.

"That's cool," Tom said, but I had the impression that he didn't think it was cool at all.

"We should go get something," I whispered to Dylan.

"Yeah."

"There's a convenience store just up the way. We could get something there," I suggested.

"I've got a better idea," Chelsea said. "Tomorrow night we'll throw a party and invite all these people to our place."

"I'm not so sure that's a good idea."

"Why not?"

"We don't know all these people."

"They don't know us and they invited us. Besides, by the time we leave, we'll know everyone. Get real, Jen. It's a holiday weekend. There should be parties every night. People could stay outside if you're worried that they'll steal something—"

"I'm not worried." Okay. I was a little.

"What do you think, Amy?" Chelsea asked.

"I think it would be okay."

That wasn't exactly a resounding endorsement of Chelsea's plan. Her okay sounded more like a hesitant "fine," like she didn't really think it was a good idea but was afraid to commit to saying so.

"Great! Two to one, we're partying at our place tomorrow night. Spread the word."

Before I could argue, Chelsea had invited Susan and Tom. We were forgiven for not bringing anything. I had a feeling that in the long run walking to a convenience store and buying a bag of chips and some drinks would have been less trouble.

My businesslike mind started planning this party that Chelsea had arranged. We could have the party outside, beneath the beach house. We could grill hot dogs. It could work.

"It'll be okay," Dylan said.

"Yeah, and fun," I said, trying to sound upbeat.

And not worry. And wondering when my friends and I had started to no longer think alike. There was a time when we'd known what the other was going to say before anyone spoke. But I'd certainly not expected Chelsea to suggest a party at our place or for Amy to blithely agree with her.

"I'll get us something to drink," Dylan said. He headed toward a line of ice chests.

"You're not mad at me, are you?" Amy asked.

"You didn't sound exactly enthused about the idea."

"It'll be a good chance to meet more people. We don't want to spend the summer completely alone."

"We're hardly doing that," I said. "We're a week into being on the island and we have Noah, Zach, and Dylan."

"Chelsea has Noah. You have Dylan. Zach is with me by default."

"That's not true."

"Yes, it is. I can see there's something special with you and Dylan. And Chelsea is all over Noah like he's made of chocolate."

I laughed. "They are pretty bad."

"Zach is nice and I like him, but we're just friends. Passing the time until he leaves."

"Has he said when they're doing that . . . leaving?" I hadn't asked Dylan because I didn't really want to know.

"No."

"Then don't ask, and don't tell me if you do ask. I just want it to happen without warning."

"That'll make it hard, Jen."

"It'll be harder if I'm counting the minutes. This way, I can pretend that there isn't an end coming."

"But there will be. Soon."

"I know, Amy. And I'll deal with it then."

"Deal with what?"

I turned to Dylan, wondering when he'd returned, how much he'd heard. Obviously not much if he didn't know what I was talking about, and I wasn't about to tell him.

"I was just saying that I'd deal with the party planning tomorrow."

"Good idea." He handed me a wine cooler and grinned. "Right now, it's party time!"

CHAPTER 20

I drank the wine cooler, because I didn't want to admit that I was too young. Besides, I wasn't *that* underage. And, for a while, the drinking age in this state had been eighteen, so back then, I would have been old enough to drink. And, if I were in Europe with my grandparents, I'd be drinking wine. Everyone drank wine over there. It sounded totally rational to me, especially by the time I finished the wine cooler.

Along with everyone else, Dylan and I were dancing on the sand. Someone had hooked up a CD player to speakers and music was blasting into the night. The fire was still going. Dylan handed me another wine cooler. I was feeling good. Really good. Totally relaxed.

The party tomorrow night was starting to

sound like a terrific idea whenever I thought about it. Which wasn't very often. Mostly I thought about Dylan. And how much I liked him, and how much I didn't want to think about him leaving.

Every now and then he'd pull me close, dance slowly with me nestled up against him. Even when the rhythm of the music was fast. Like we were dancing to a song that only he could hear. Then he'd release me and we'd be dancing again to the same music as everyone else.

It was nearly midnight when he pulled me close again, rubbed his cheek against mine, his mouth near my ear. I could feel his warm breath against my neck.

"I've had way too many beers," he said.

"Me, too."

"You didn't have any beers."

"Wine coolers, then. Too many wine coolers."

"You know what I've always wanted to do?"

I shook my head.

"Swim in the ocean at night."

"It's too dark. You can't see what's out there."

"Nothing's in the ocean at night that's not there during the day."

I jerked my head back. "Are you crazy? Have you seen *Jaws*?"

"*Jaws 1, 2,* and *3-D*. Like I said, there's nothing in the water at night that's not there during the day. Let's go swim."

"I'm not wearing my bathing suit."

He grinned. "Neither am I."

Be bold, Jennifer, I thought.

"What about Amy and Chelsea—"

"They won't miss us."

Chelsea definitely wouldn't, but Amy . . . she'd be fine. She had Zach and her dog. And I had Dylan. For only a short time.

"Okay." I sounded breathless, nervous, scared, and excited. Because I was all those things. And a little lightheaded, a little disoriented.

Dylan swung his arm around me, nestled my face into the nook of his shoulder. We started walking, stepping on each other's feet, laughing. Until we finally moved apart and settled for holding hands. Walking away from the fire and the light. Back toward the end of the island where our beach house was.

The moon and stars and distant houses cast

a pale light over the island. Everything felt different. The sand beneath the soles of my feet, the whisper of the wind off the ocean.

"I've never had a wine cooler before," I confessed.

"Are you drunk?" Dylan asked.

"I don't think so. How would I know?"

"You'd know."

"I feel good. Relaxed."

"Me, too."

"Are you drunk?"

"No."

"It wouldn't be smart to go in the water if you're drunk."

"I'm not drunk."

In the shadows, I could see him studying me as we walked along the shoreline, the water occasionally rolling in around our feet.

"You worry about a lot of things, don't you?" he asked.

He didn't sound critical. Simply stating an observation.

"I like to be responsible. The beach house is my grandparents'. They trusted me with it."

"And you're taking good care of it."

"I'm trying."

"That's all they can expect."

He drew me up close and his mouth met mine, neither of us hesitating, both of us obviously ready. The kiss was lazy, like the one we'd shared last night. No hurry. Like he had no plans to leave. Like we had all the time in the world. I felt like warm honey was moving through my veins.

"I've wanted to do that all night," he said when he pulled back.

"I thought you wanted to go swimming."

"Hey, I can want more than one thing at a time."

He kissed me again, and I thought maybe we wouldn't go swimming after all. Maybe we'd just stand here for the remainder of the night while the tide flowed in . . . until morning, when the tide flowed out.

He stepped away, and I almost followed him so I could stay nestled up against him, like metal to a magnet.

"Okay. Okay," he said. "Need to do this before I'm thinking straight again and decide this might be a bad idea."

"What's a bad idea?"

"Swimming at night."

"So now you agree with me?"

I could see that he was facing the water, his hands on his hips. There was enough light to make out shadows and shapes.

"I really want to do this."

I watched as he pulled his shirt over his head. He dropped it to the ground. "I really don't want to do it alone. We'll be safe as long as we're together."

That sounded so incredibly romantic. Of course, Leonardo DiCaprio and Kate Winslet had thought the same thing in *Titanic*. And look how that had ended.

Still, I took a deep breath to shore up my resolve and my courage, my spirit of adventure. "Okay."

He grabbed my hand, and we ran into the sea.

CHAPTER 21

I loved it!

The water was warmer than I expected, and whenever the waves crashed against us, Dylan pulled me nearer, protectively, shielding me as much as he could from the power of the ocean. He was warmer than the water. And strong. And firm. His skin felt wonderful, silky, slick.

My shorts and tank top were plastered against me. The water was swirling around my waist. Suddenly I felt something hard beneath my foot. Felt it move.

"Oh!" I jumped up in the water. "I think I stepped on a crab!"

"It's probably the brother of the one you dumped in the boiling water."

"I didn't dump him! You did."

He laughed. "Get on my back."

I didn't hesitate. I climbed on, wrapping my legs around his waist, my arms around his neck. He hooked his arms beneath my knees.

"This is fun," I said, "but it's not really swimming."

"Close enough. I like it better anyway."

I tightened my hold. "Aren't you afraid something might snap at you?"

"I'm tough."

He walked farther out, until the water reached his chest and the waves weren't as big or as strong. I laid my head on Dylan's shoulder and thought I could go to sleep right there.

"Jennifer, what are you going to do when the summer ends?"

"Go to school at the university in Austin." I didn't have to ask what he'd be doing, because I knew and it scared me a little.

"I'm going to major in business," I added, anything to stop myself from thinking about what he was going to be doing.

"Are you going to join a sorority?"

"Nah, too girly-girl. Chelsea probably will, but not me."

I kissed Dylan's bare shoulder. Although I'd asked last night, and he'd avoided a truthful answer, since he was asking personal questions, I decided to try again. "Why the army, Dylan?"

"I have a Rambo complex."

"What's that mean?"

"I want to be Rambo."

He sprung forward, twisted. I shrieked, just before we both went under the water. I came up sputtering and mad at him for tricking me. He was laughing. I was treading water, really not wanting my feet to touch the sand in case the crab was still around.

"What did you do that for?" I asked.

"We were getting too serious. And I'm getting sober and tired. Let's get back to shore."

We swam toward shore, the waves pushing us. Body surfing more than swimming. When the water became shallow, I let my feet touch the bottom, and then I ran out of the water. I plopped down on my back on the wet sand. The ocean rolled around me, and I could feel the sand shifting beneath me. It felt really strange. Dylan dropped down beside me.

"My reasons for going into the army aren't heroic, Jen. I tried college, didn't like it. I've got no skills. The army will let me play with guns."

He was lying on his side, raised up on an elbow. I reached up and touched his cheek. "Rambo."

"Yeah."

"Are you scared?"

"Sometimes. But it's the kind of scared we felt going into the ocean just now. You can't really see what's out there, and what we imagined in our mind was scarier than the reality."

"I thought there would be a shark," I confessed.

He lay on his back and wrapped his hand around mine. "No sharks."

I looked up at the black, black sky and all the stars. I was suddenly feeling very, very tired. Spent. As though the long day and night were catching up with me.

"You get a day off from the campground?"

I yawned, rolled over onto my side, and studied the silhouette of his face. "Wednesday."

"Want to spend the day with me?"

"Sure. I could get us a sailboat from the marina. We could go sailing in the lagoon, go out and have a picnic in the cove. Someplace special."

"Do you know how to sail?"

"Yeah. And I can teach you."

"Okay, Wednesday, then, we'll go sailing."

"Definitely."

Then he rolled over, half on me, half off. I loved the weight of his body over mine, and more, I loved the way his mouth moved over mine as he kissed me, deeply. I felt like I was back in the ocean, terrified, exhilarated, frightened, excited. Exactly where I wanted to be, doing exactly what I wanted to be doing.

CHAPTER 22

I dragged myself out of bed the next morning, my head feeling swollen to twice its normal size. I remembered Dylan walking me back home. I remembered crawling into bed. I remembered sleeping like the dead. And I so wished I didn't have to go to work.

Now I was sounding like Chelsea, which until this summer I'd never minded. I mean, we often sounded like each other. But I'd never before noticed all the ways that we were different. While she didn't like working, I did. Not the everyday grind, of course. But the satisfaction of doing a good job and getting paid for it. Especially the getting paid for it part.

I went into the bathroom and turned on the shower. When the water was hot enough,

I stepped beneath the spray, hoping the heat would shrink my head back to its normal size. Was this how it felt to have a hangover?

I didn't think I'd had that much to drink, but I felt so sluggish. If it wasn't the wine coolers working their way through my system, then I was getting seriously sick. I let the water beat down on me until the water started coming through lukewarm. Oops!

I quickly shut it off. Amy wasn't going to appreciate that the water would turn cold on her so quickly. I stepped out of the shower, dried off, wrapped one towel around my body and another turban-style around my head. The bathroom was misty, the mirror foggy, so I decided to go to my room to dry my hair and get dressed. I opened the door and staggered to a stop, staring at some freckle-faced stranger. I clutched the towel tighter.

"Hey," he said, grinning. "Amy said I could use the shower."

"Oh."

"I'm Alex."

"Oh."

"You're Jennifer, right?"

"Right."

"Yeah, Amy told me all about you. This house is way cool."

"Thanks." What do you say to a guy you don't know when nothing separates you except a towel?

"Later," he said.

He squeezed past me and closed the door. Okay, that was weird. I scampered into my room, dried my hair, left it loose, and got dressed as quickly as I could. Then I went across the hallway and knocked on Amy's door. "Amy?"

"Down here!"

I went down the stairs and into the kitchen. She was scrambling eggs.

"There is a guy using our shower."

"Yeah. Alex. I met him last night."

"Why does he need to use our shower?"

"Because he stinks."

"I got that. I mean, why doesn't he have a shower?"

"He's working on the island but he can't afford to rent any place so he's been sleeping in his car. He'll help with the groceries."

"What do you mean?"

"In exchange for using the shower."

"You say that like this is a permanent arrangement."

She shrugged. "We have the extra room."

"But he's not on the contract we signed with my grandparents."

"Neither is Noah."

"I'm not believing this." I plowed my hands through my hair. "Y'all can't just invite people to live here."

"I'm being charitable."

I heard a mewling sound, glanced in the corner, and saw a cat drinking from a bowl of milk. "What is that?"

"A cat."

"I know that. I mean why is it here?"

"Alex and I found it last night on the way home."

"Amy, you can't pick up every stray you find."

"I won't. This is it. A dog and a cat."

"And a guy. Don't forget the guy who nearly gave me a heart attack when I stepped into the hallway."

"If you hadn't stayed out so late, I would

have introduced you last night. Where were you, anyway? You and Dylan disappeared."

"We went swimming."

"In the ocean? At night? Do you know how dangerous that is?"

"No more dangerous than letting some guy you don't know sleep in the house."

"Noah would protect us."

"Yeah, I saw how Noah came to our rescue when I discovered the dog. He's going to be a big help in a crisis."

Amy dumped the eggs onto a plate. "Here. Go ahead and eat. You and I need to get to work."

What was wrong with that sentence?

"Where's Chelsea?"

"She's not feeling well. She's not going to work today."

"What's wrong with her?" Was it the summer flu? Was I coming down with it as well? Was that why my head felt stuffed?

"Nothing serious. She said she needs an attitude adjustment."

"In other words, she just doesn't want to go to work."

"Yeah, but let it go, Jen. You're not her mother."

"I got her the job."

"So? You don't have to tell Mrs. Plackette that Chelsea is mentally sick, not physically sick."

"I feel like I don't even know who she is."

"She's our best friend."

But a best friend doesn't leave you in a lurch, and she's not supposed to care more about being with her boyfriend than being loyal to you.

"Besides, she can spend today getting things ready for tonight," Amy said.

Right. Tonight. The big party.

I should have let it go, should have left right then. Instead I marched to Chelsea's bedroom and banged on the door. "Chelsea! Chelsea! We need to talk!"

She flung open the door and stood there in her shorty pajamas, hands on her hips, glaring at me. Her hair had a tousled look that I figured Noah had designed.

"Do you mind? We're sleeping here."

"You're not going to work?"

"Amy was supposed to tell you."

"Why didn't you?"

"Because you're not the boss of me."

How juvenile did that sound? "Mrs. P—"

"Is cool with me not coming in today. I already called. So chill."

She started to close the door. I flattened my hand against it. "About this party tonight—"

"I'll take care of it. It's the reason I called in sick. There's a lot to be done, and this way you don't have to worry about it."

Yeah, right. Concern for me was the motive.

"No one comes inside the house," I stated firmly.

She rolled her eyes. "Of course not. Relax. You can depend on me."

"This from someone who just called in sick when she isn't?"

"Like I said. You're not the boss of me. Now get your hand off my door."

"All right! Cat fight!" Noah called from the bed. "You go, Chels."

Reflex had me looking past her to the bed. I saw more of Noah than I ever wanted to see. At that moment, I hated the guy.

"It's not a cat fight," I said. I looked back at Chelsea. "I'm just really disappointed in you, Chels."

"Same goes."

What was happening between us? I dropped my hand to my side. Chelsea slammed the door shut, reigniting my anger.

"I mean it, Chelsea! No strangers in the house! You'd better not do anything that my grandparents would consider wild!" Although I was pretty sure she'd already done that by having a guy in her bed. They were old-fashioned.

I walked back into the kitchen. Amy was wiping down the counter. She'd cleaned up everything except my plate of eggs. But I had no appetite. I dumped the eggs into the disposal, rinsed the plate, and put it in the dishwasher.

"I guess we need to go. Are you dropping Alex off somewhere?"

"Actually, I told him that he could crash in the extra bedroom while we're gone."

Great. Just great.

Amy was driving to the campground before we spoke again.

"It'll be all right, Jen. The sun is out so the campground shouldn't be too busy. It's just maintenance today. No big deal."

"I just thought we'd all be hanging out together, having fun."

"We are hanging out together."

I shifted around in my seat, gave the back an exaggerated look-see. "I see only two of us here."

"So today is an exception. We can't be together 24/7. Besides, I bet you'll want to spend some time alone with Dylan this evening."

I felt the heat rush to my face. I suppose I was being a little unfair, because not only did I want time with Dylan this evening, but I wanted time alone with him on my day off. So, okay, Amy had a point, and maybe Chelsea was right in wanting to spend time with Noah. I just hadn't expected it to be like this.

We pulled into the campground, and Amy parked in the parking area. As we got out, I looked between the main building and the Beach Hut. I could see the beach that ran along the bay and Dylan's tent. It was clearly visible between a motor home and travel trailer parked on sites side by side.

I had an irrational urge to pull a Chelsea, to tell Amy that I wasn't feeling well, to walk down to the beach, and spend the day with Dylan. Two more days and that's exactly what I would do.

CHAPTER 23

The hours slowly ticked by. The campground was full and we had no registrations to take care of, so I spent most of the day restocking drinks and souvenirs. Even though we didn't really need Chelsea around, it didn't lessen my irritation with her.

I thought about what Amy had said. I wasn't Chelsea's mother. Still, I found myself wondering if I was even her friend.

By the time Amy and I got home, the party was in full swing.

"Where did all these people come from?" Amy asked as she stopped the car.

I estimated over two dozen people engaged in various activities. Most wore bathing suits. Some stood around the grill, some were playing volleyball—I had no idea where the net had come from—some were dancing, some were hooking up on the balcony.

The balcony! They weren't supposed to be in the house.

"There are people on the balcony," I said in disbelief.

"So?"

"This was supposed to be an outside party."

"The balcony is outside."

I glared at Amy. "To get onto the balcony, they had to be inside at some point."

"Hey, don't get pissed at me. I had nothing to do with any of this. I was at work all day."

She was right. She was so right.

"Why have I never noticed before that Chelsea simply does as she pleases?"

"It does seem like she suddenly thinks that no rules apply to her," Amy said. "Maybe it's a freedom thing. I've heard some people go wild when they move away from home."

"This is beyond wild. This is . . ." I growled. I didn't know what this was.

I climbed out of the car. As Amy and I walked to the house, people greeted us like we were old friends. I didn't recognize a single one of them.

Inside the house even more people were hanging around: in the kitchen, in the living room. What had Chelsea done?

Then I spotted Dylan playing Ping-Pong with Zach. When he saw me, he grinned.

It was crazy, irrational, but suddenly I didn't care about Chelsea's irresponsibility or the fact that all these people were here. I only cared that Dylan was.

I walked over to him. He bounced the ball on the table, and caught it.

"This massive crowd was unexpected," I said.

"Yeah."

"Who are all these people?"

He shrugged. "They just started showing up. Word seemed to travel fast that a party was going on here."

"I promised my grandparents we wouldn't have any wild parties."

"It's not really wild."

But it got that way. Someone showed up with a keg of beer. The music got louder as the night got darker. It served as a siren not for the police but for more people. It was almost as if the whole island was standing around in our yard.

I guess my stress level began to show, because Dylan and Zach helped me convince people that the true party was happening outside, not inside. And once strangers were no longer in my grandparents' house, I began to feel a little better about having all these people over.

I figured if we were really disturbing the peace, the Coast Guard would pull up in the water beside the house and tell us to break it up.

But no one came along to stop the festivities. Hot dogs were roasting on the grill. Before we'd chased everyone out of the house, crabs and shrimp had been boiled in the kitchen.

"We should do this every night," Chelsea said, showing up on the balcony unexpectedly. I was sitting there with Dylan, watching the stars come out.

"People just arrived, bringing food and drinks," she continued. "We haven't had to spend a single penny. Isn't this just the greatest?"

"Do you even know any of these people?" I asked.

"Sure. I've met some of them. It's like one of those e-mail chain letters. You send it to six of your friends who send it to six of their friends and it multiplies into infinity. You should understand that. It's a math concept. When you're finished, you have all these people coming together—"

"No, you end up with an inbox full of spam."

"When did you become such a downer?"

"I'm not. I just don't want to do this every night."

"You're just jealous because it was my idea and it's gone over so well."

I stared after her as she disappeared into her bedroom.

"Chelsea!" I finally called when my brain unfroze.

I got up and turned the door knob. She'd locked it. "Chelsea!"

"It's not important," Dylan said.

"How do you know what's important and what isn't?" I asked, not bothering to hide my irritation.

He held up his hands. "Fine. It's important." He looked back toward the stars.

Whoa! Were we having our first fight?

I sat down in the chair. "I'm sorry."

He shifted his attention back to me. I felt a desperate need to explain. "Chelsea has been my best friend forever, but living with her is a . . . challenge. This summer, it's like an alien took possession of her or something. Do you and Zach have trouble living together?"

"No. Must be a chick thing."

"And you're sexist."

"I'm sexy."

"You're that, too, but you're trying to change the subject. Chelsea and I arguing is not a chick thing." Was it?

"Zach does his thing, I do mine. Maybe you and Chelsea spend too much time together."

"That was the whole point of us living together on the island this summer. To do things together, because we won't be together in the fall. But we're not spending any time together. It's like I hardly see her, except at work."

"Why don't you worry about spending time with Chelsea *after* I leave?"

It was like he threw a cold bucket of water on me. What was I thinking to be sitting here arguing about something so trivial? He was going to be gone in a few days; I'd never see him again. Why was I letting Chelsea ruin my time with Dylan, ruin my summer?

Dylan was right. My problems weren't his concern. I wasn't going to have with Dylan what Chelsea had with Noah. And that was okay. Because I didn't want commitment. I wanted a summer of fun with my best buds.

Dylan was an unexpected surprise, and when he left I'd get back on track with Chelsea.

I nodded. "You're right. Let's go have some fun."

We went outside where the music was playing and the beer was flowing. We danced with each other. We danced with strangers. We danced when no one seemed to be able to tell who was partnered with whom.

I lost sight of Dylan. I lost sight of Amy. I lost sight of Chelsea. It was just me and all these strangers; people I didn't really know, people who had shown up because they'd heard a good time was happening at our end of the island, on our bit of private land.

I was suddenly overwhelmed, wondering if this was what college would be like. A place with no familiar faces, hundreds and hundreds of strangers walking past me, bumping into me. I didn't know what to say to these people. What did we have in common?

Nothing except the desire to have a good time.

What did they know about me? Nothing.

Yes, I thought. This was what college would be like. It would be like starting over, like kindergarten. Only my mom wouldn't walk with me into the classroom. I'd be stepping onto the campus all by myself.

It was what I wanted. It truly was, but suddenly the idea of being surrounded by all these people that I didn't know . . .

I saw the light go on in Chelsea's room. Saw it go out. She was in there with Noah, probably clinging to him. Maybe she was as terrified as I was with all the changes. Maybe Noah was her haven, her refuge.

But where was mine?

An arm wound around my waist, and I was

pulled up against a body. I lifted my gaze . . . Dylan.

He grinned. "Thought I'd lost you."

I shook my head. "No, I was here."

He pulled me closer, rubbed his cheek against mine.

"Don't go to work tomorrow," he whispered. His voice was low, sultry like the night.

"I have to. We'll be so busy with people leaving—"

"We don't have much time left. I want to spend it with you."

My heart was pounding. I felt like I was teetering on the edge of a cliff. I'd always been so damned responsible.

Chelsea had called in sick when she wasn't. She'd still have a job tomorrow. She'd had no punishment. She'd been outside for most of the afternoon and evening and lightning hadn't struck her.

"Please," he said, nuzzling my neck.

And that was all it took for me to fall off the ledge.

"Okay."

CHAPTER 24

I felt wickedly wonderful. Not a shred of guilt. Okay. There was a shred of guilt pricking my conscience, but I told myself that I would make it up to Mrs. P. I'd work a day when I really was sick. Go in with a headache or cramps or a fever. So I was sorta taking an advance on a sick day. At least, that's how I rationalized it.

I called Mrs. P as soon as I woke up, before I'd used my voice so it sounded low, raspy—hopefully making me sound like I was truly ill. And hopefully so she wouldn't notice on her end that my voice was shaking on my end. The fact that I had a slight headache from drinking the night before also eased my guilt. I was kinda sorta a little bit sick.

And I felt a lot worse when I went into the

kitchen and saw the mess from the party. It had been so late when everyone finally left, and we'd been wiped out. So we hadn't bothered to wash the dishes that had somehow managed to get used—even though we'd put out paper plates and cups. We'd just stacked everything on the counters and island.

The cat was on the counter, lapping up beer that had spilled out of an overturned mug. Tiny was gnawing on a partial hot dog. But that wasn't the worst of it.

Two large trash cans had been overturned, their contents spread over the kitchen. I could see the large, hairy back end of a strange dog sticking out of one of the cans.

Another dog, huge and mangy looking, had its paws on the island and was licking ketchup off a plate. The plate tottered, and before I could reach it, or even decide if I should approach the beast, the plate hit the floor and shattered.

"Amy!" I walked into the hallway. "Amy!" I shrieked at the top of my lungs.

Footsteps sounded on the stairs. A heavy-set guy with a beard and a dirty T-shirt that said

DESIGNATED DRINKER stopped in front of me.

"What's wrong?" he asked.

"Amy!"

I heard softer footsteps on the stairs and a door open behind me. Amy and Chelsea reached me at the same time.

"What is wrong with you?" Chelsea asked.

"Amy's strays. Let's start with this guy. I don't know him," I said, looking at Designated Drinker.

"He drank too much and was just sleeping it off," Amy said. "He's not permanent."

"And the two new dogs? Are they sleeping it off?"

Amy had the grace to blush. "No, they're really strays. We have to keep them, Jen."

"Have you *looked* in the kitchen recently?"

She cautiously eased past me and peered around the corner. "Shit."

"Exactly."

I looked at Designated Drinker. "Did you sleep on a bed?"

"Top bunk."

"Wash the sheets before you go."

Alex had crept down the stairs, and Noah

was standing behind Chelsea, yawning and scratching his head.

I took a second to look at everyone, and then I said very firmly, "I want this mess cleaned up now."

"You're not the boss—"

"Right now, I am," I said, cutting Chelsea off. "This is *my* grandparents' house, and we promised to take care of it. We have one hour to make this house look as clean as it did the day we arrived. Or else."

"Or else what?"

"We move back home."

It was a threat I never would have carried out. I didn't think. I mean, I wanted to be here as much—if not more—than they did. And my parents would never agree to let me stay here all alone.

But they didn't know that.

Which might be why they pitched in with such enthusiasm. All of them. Even Designated Drinker. It took us almost two hours. It didn't help that the dogs kept trying to retrieve what we put in the trash. Noah finally took them outside, along with a bottle of Chelsea's strawberry-scented shampoo. She started to protest, looked at me, and went back to scrubbing the counters.

We were further slowed by the fact that we had to keep stepping around a drunken cat. It actually staggered, this way and that. And in the end was what lightened the mood and got us all to laugh again.

Until it barfed.

But even then, things didn't seem quite so bad. We had the dishes cleaned and put away, the counters scrubbed, the floors swept and mopped, linens washed. The dogs smelling like Chelsea. Which I thought was funny as well.

I waited until we were finished putting everything back to the way it was and Designated Drinker left before I confessed my plans for the day to Amy and Chelsea. After all, they needed to know so they could back up my story.

"You gave me all that grief about taking a day off, and now you've called in sick?" Chelsea asked. "Have you got a lot of nerve or what?"

I knew I deserved that, but I'd hoped she'd be a bit more mature about it.

"It's not the same thing, Chelsea. You have

Noah every day. Dylan is going to be leaving. I'll probably never see him again."

"That's so weak, Jen. At least I was spending the day with someone I love. You're taking a sick day to be with someone who doesn't care enough about you to hang around. He's using you. He's like a sailor. A girl in every port."

"He's not using me," I said defiantly. "We have something special."

"Right."

It really ticked me off that she'd put all these doubts out there to mingle with my guilt over lying to Mrs. P. Sure, Dylan and I weren't committed to each other, and he might have a girl in every port—or at least on every island . . . I didn't want to think about it. I didn't want to question my actions today or his actions in the future. I didn't want to speculate about what was really happening between us—or not happening. Or why he wouldn't stick around.

I stood on the balcony and watched Amy and Chelsea drive away and tried not to feel the guilt settling in the pit of my stomach or the doubts weaving through my heart.

But when Dylan arrived, the guilt and doubts

fled as quickly as they'd arrived. I was so incredibly glad to see him, so glad that I'd agreed to play hooky today. Really, who would it hurt? Most of the campers had left late yesterday. It would be the weekend before we were busy again . . . but I didn't want to think about that. I just wanted to think about my time with Dylan.

I would have loved to have time alone with him in the house, cuddling on the couch, sitting on the balcony, but Noah and the shower guy—Alex—were hanging out together, watching some show about surfing. Like they'd ever surf. It would require getting off their butts. And I didn't see that happening any time soon.

I was decked out in my bikini. I grabbed my beach bag and jogged down the steps. I refused to let the fact that this summer wasn't what I'd envisioned bring me down.

I was going to spend the day with Dylan.

I stepped out into the sunlight. He was waiting for me. He slipped his arm around me, his hand warm against my bare side.

"Where's your stuff?" I asked.

"I travel light."

"Hold on then. I'll be right back. I've got

another beach towel."

I ran back up the stairs and into my bedroom, grabbed another beach towel, and an extra bottle of lotion. Stopped off in the kitchen and tossed some extra drinks into my bag, along with some snacks.

Then an idea hit me. I walked into the living room. It didn't appear that either Noah or Alex had moved a muscle.

"Noah?"

He was lying on the couch. He craned his neck back to look at me, somehow keeping half his gaze on the TV. "Yeah?"

Nothing ventured, nothing gained. I took a deep breath.

"I was wondering if you guys could make yourselves scarce around noon. I'd like some alone time with Dylan here in the house."

He wiggled his eyebrows suggestively. "I bet you do, but relax. I hear nothing, see nothing, speak nothing."

I sighed. So typical of a guy to not get what I wanted. "I just want to fix him lunch, but I'd like nothing to distract us."

"I'm down with that. I'll make myself scarce."

"Alex?"

"I'm already gone."

"Will you take the animals with you as well?"

"Sure thing," Noah said. "That's what roomies do, right? Help each other out."

"If you really wanted to help out, you could chip in on the expenses and the daily chores."

"Chelsea said everything was covered."

"Yeah. By us." I waved my hand. "Never mind. Just be gone by noon."

"Not a problem."

The beach was paved with bodies—every shape, size, and skin tone. But since Dylan and I headed down to the sand early, we'd managed to grab some prime real estate. On the soft sand, near the water.

We'd staked our claim with a beach umbrella and our beach towels covering the sand. We'd slathered lotion over each other, and then we'd talked. About nothing. About everything.

He had two older brothers, both in the army. Special Forces. So he was feeling the pressure to measure up. Neither of us wanted to really dwell on the dangers . . . or the fact that he might be going far away.

Instead I told him about the drunken cat that morning. He laughed. A wonderful, marvelous laugh.

He told me about the first night that he and Zach camped out.

"We just headed out from home, no plans at all, except to reach the northeast corner of the Texas coast. We got there just as it was getting dark. Nothing in sight. Nothing. Just sand and water. No houses, no lights, no people. So we set up our tent, right there on the beach. Cooked supper over a driftwood fire. Real adventurers. Do you have any idea how dark it gets at night when there isn't a town nearby?"

"Pitch black?"

"Blacker. But the stars. They're beautiful, Jennifer. No city lights to fade them. You feel so small."

We were on our sides, facing each other. He played with my hair while he talked, wrapping strands around his finger, unwrapping them.

"Were you scared?" I asked.

"Nah, not really. Just in awe that we could

be so insignificant."

"You're not insignificant."

"Not like I didn't matter . . . it's just that everything else seems so much greater. We hardly talked at all. Just communed with nature. The next morning nature communed with us. The tide came in and soaked us. We'd pitched our tent too close to the water."

I laughed. "You're kidding!"

"Nope. Made a mess of everything."

"I thought tents were waterproof."

"Not when you leave it unzipped so you can have a breeze blowing inside." He tugged on my hair. "You ever slept in a tent?"

"No. I know it's odd for a person who works at a campground not to like camping, but I like having air-conditioning and a bathroom."

"I'd like you to sleep in my tent sometime."

"I've seen your tent. It's tiny. I think three would be a crowd."

"Zach hooked up with an island girl at the party last night. I'm sleeping solo until we leave."

"Oh."

That one little word seemed to say nothing

and everything. I swallowed hard, thinking that I should follow it with something significant.

"Will you think about keeping me company in my tent?"

I nodded. Yeah, I could think about it. As a matter of fact, now that he'd put the notion in my mind, I wasn't certain that I could think about anything else.

CHAPTER 25

While I puttered around in the kitchen fixing lunch, I couldn't get two thoughts out of my head: that Dylan had extended a not-so-subtle invitation to sleep with him, and that Chelsea might be right, darn her. Dylan and Zach were trying to hook up with girls on every island.

I wanted to believe that I was special. That he'd planned to spend only a day or two on this island and had hung around longer because he really liked me.

"So where's Noah?" he asked.

"He had things to do."

Dylan was sitting on the bench seat at the table by the window, his arm stretched across the back, watching me. Usually, I didn't mind guys watching me. All right. I'm a normal girl. I *like* guys watching me. It's why I spend time making my hair look stylishly messy and putting on makeup. It's why I always wear clothes that leave my pierced belly button visible.

What girl doesn't want the attention of a guy?

But Dylan wasn't watching me like he was intrigued or fascinated. He was watching me like he was baffled.

I was standing at the wooden island in the center of the kitchen, chopping up chicken breast, celery, onions, and walnuts to make Gran's famous chicken salad. I was trying really hard not to feel his gaze on me.

But I felt it anyway.

"What's wrong?" he asked.

"Nothing."

How could I explain what I didn't understand?

"What about that other guy who lives here now?"

"Same thing. He had things to do."

"You in tight with him?"

I swung around. "No. He's Amy's friend." I

shrugged. "Or something. She acts like this place is a shelter, offering anything we have to any stray that shows up."

He was studying me again, his blue gaze intense.

"I can see the dolphins," he said, a total change in subject. I welcomed it.

I walked to the refrigerator and took out a head of lettuce. "I love watching them."

Chopped it up, washed it. Put a little on two plates. Then using an ice-cream scoop, I gathered up the chicken salad and put a nice little mound on top of the lettuce.

"Or maybe they're porpoises," he said.

"Maybe. I never can tell the difference."

I washed off strawberries and put them around the mound. I thought it looked very artistic.

I set a plate before Dylan and one opposite him. I got the box of saltines out of the pantry and put it on the table. I'd already poured two glasses of sweetened tea and left the pitcher within easy reach. I slid onto the bench and smiled. "Dig in."

"Do you have bread?"

"Oh, yeah."

I retrieved the bread, watched as he turned my creation into a sandwich, leaving only the strawberries on the plate.

"I've never been much for salads," he said. He took a bite of his sandwich. "It's good."

"It's my grandma's recipe."

With my fork, I started picking at the chicken, wondering if I should have chopped it up finer. It didn't look exactly the way Gran's salad did. I scooped some up and ate it.

"Is it because I said that I want to sleep with you?"

I almost choked. I took a sip of tea, trying to get the chicken salad to go down my suddenly knotted-up throat. It was dry. Way too dry.

I swallowed, cleared my throat. "That isn't exactly what you said. You said you wanted me to sleep in your tent."

"Yeah, in my tent *with me.* But you're not down with that."

I looked at him, studying him the way he'd been studying me. "I don't know. I've thought about it." A lot. Wondered, agonized, tried to figure out where we were going here.

"But . . . " His voice trailed off.

"When you leave here, will I ever see you again?"

He looked around the kitchen, looked out the window like he was trying to find the answer. Finally, he brought his gaze back to me. "Probably not."

I nodded. "And when you leave here, you'll meet other girls and maybe invite them into your tent. Maybe there was a girl before you got here."

"There wasn't."

"But there will be after you leave." It was a statement, but it sounded like a question, and I was hoping he'd deny it.

"Probably."

I gave him points for being honest. But points only count in sports.

He sat back against the bench. "Look, Jennifer, that's what my summer is all about. Camping along the coast. Meeting girls, partying, drinking. Having a grand, final send-off."

"I know, and I understand. I just don't want to be one of the girls. For me to sleep with a guy, I have to be *the* girl. The *only* girl."

He gave me a funny, lopsided grin and looked out the window. Like he didn't know how to respond to my heartfelt declaration. Like he hadn't expected me to say no to his invitation.

To be honest, I hadn't thought I'd say no either. And if Chelsea hadn't given me a reality check with her talk about all the girls in various ports, I probably wouldn't have.

"I'm sorry if you feel like your time with me has been wasted," I said quietly.

He slid his gaze over to me, reached across the table, and took my hand. "I don't feel that way. Sure, I'm disappointed. Sure, I'd hoped for more. But I can respect where you're coming from. Doesn't mean I like it, but I can respect it."

"So what now? Are you going out in search of an island girl for tonight?"

"I'm not trying to put notches in my tent pole. I just want to have a blast this summer. I have fun when I'm with you. So for now, you're the only island girl I want to spend time with."

CHAPTER 26

I was in the bathroom getting ready for my big date. After lunch, Dylan and I had returned to the beach for a little while. We'd played in the surf, stretched out on our blankets on the sand. And spent a good deal of time kissing.

Tomorrow I'd follow through on the promise I'd made to him earlier, about getting a sailboat from the marina. We couldn't do it today, obviously. Because I was supposed to be sick.

Tonight we were going to party at some of the clubs on the island. I wanted to make sure that Dylan's eyes never strayed from me. Although he'd repeatedly slathered lotion on me through the afternoon, I looked as though I'd been in the sun all day, a very pale pinkish hue. To enhance the island girl look, I used a light bronze eye shadow and a shimmery, tawny blush. I was leaning over the sink, close to the mirror, applying mascara when the door suddenly burst open. I slashed the tip of the mascara brush across my forehead, leaving a black line. Great. Just great.

"Are you happy now?"

Chelsea stood there looking seriously peeved.

"Well, yeah," I answered. After all, I was going to spend time this evening with Dylan. Why wouldn't I be happy?

"Because you know you're a real bitch, butting in where you have absolutely no business."

Whoa!

"I'm totally lost here, Chels."

"Noah got a job."

I stared at her. "What?"

"This afternoon. He's going to work as a waiter at the Sandpiper. At night! And I work during the day. We'll never see each other. And it's all your fault! Why did you tell him that he needed to help out with the expenses?"

"I didn't tell him . . ." I stopped. Remembered our conversation that morning when I asked him to give me some privacy during lunch. I leaned my hip against the sink. "I wasn't issuing a command or anything. I was simply reacting to something he said. With a quick comeback line. It didn't mean anything."

"Well, it meant something to him. He thinks you think he's a bum. And he's pissed at me for not telling him that we were paying for everything."

"Who did he think was paying?"

She tucked her arms across her chest defensively and shifted her stance. "I told him the summer here was a graduation gift from our parents. That we were only working at the campground to help out some friends of yours."

"You lied to him! No wonder he's mad."

"I just wanted us to have this summer together. Now you've ruined it. You've been jealous ever since Noah came into my life."

"I'm not jealous."

"Just because I have a boyfriend and you don't."

"Excuse me? I'm cool with you having a boyfriend. I want you to be happy—"

"Then keep your nose out of my business!"

She slammed the door. I could hear her stomping down the stairs. I couldn't believe this. But I had to admit that a part of me was glad that Noah was going to start contributing his share. It wasn't fair that we were divvying up the expenses between three when four of us lived here. Well, five, now that Alex was around. I probably needed to talk with Amy to make sure that he was contributing, too.

There was a soft knock. "Jen?"

"Come on in, Amy." Why not? It was Grand Central Station around here.

She opened the door slightly and peered inside. "Have we got serious PMS going on around here?"

"Apparently."

"Are you two going to be fighting all summer?"

"We weren't fighting. She just blames me because Noah got a job."

"What's wrong with Noah getting a job? That's terrific. He can help with the expenses."

"My thoughts exactly. But he's working at night—"

"And Chelsea works during the day. Bummer."

"This so was not how I planned for our summer to go."

I heard the roar of a motorcycle arriving. Dylan.

Amy grinned. "Let it all go, Jen. Don't think about it. Chelsea will calm down eventually, and she'll see that it's all a good thing. Tonight, just have fun."

"I intend to."

I wasn't going to think about Amy's strays or Chelsea's tantrums every time something didn't go her way. I was going to spend tonight thinking only about me . . . me and Dylan.

We ended up at a club right on the beach. The windows were open and the breeze was blowing through. We could see the sunset. And with the promise of night came the promise of something more. I couldn't explain it.

Dylan was so hot. Not dressed up, of course. His black T-shirt, stretching across his shoulders, was tucked into his snug jeans.

I was in low-cut jeans. My striped top

stopped just above my waist. The area at the shoulders was cut away so my shoulders and a small portion of my arms were bared. It made me feel sexy. But not as sexy as he was.

It wasn't fair that he could look this hot with so little effort. I'd spent hours getting ready. And he'd probably done nothing more than shower and throw on his clothes.

A live band was playing in the corner. Tables were scattered around the area where people were dancing. We were sitting by the window. As shadows crept into the room, the lights remained low. It was romantic, like something from an old movie.

"What are you going to do after college?" he asked.

I laughed. "I have no idea. I need to get through it first."

"Take a guess."

"I'll work for some company, start out in management and work my way up to CEO."

"You're ambitious. Will you be on the island during the summers?"

I wondered if he was asking because he was thinking of coming back.

"Probably. I like it here. It's so relaxed."

Except when Chelsea and I were at odds, but I wasn't going to think about that. Not tonight.

"I love hanging out at the beach," he said.

"And you're going to go all the way down the Texas coast?" I knew the answer, but I was hoping maybe he'd changed his mind. Maybe he'd say, "No, I've decided to just stay here."

"All the way," he said.

I fought not to let my disappointment show.

"I've been planning it for years," he continued. "Bumming along the coast. Seeing what there is to see. Meeting people."

"You'd think one stretch of beach would look pretty much like the next." I was beginning to sound desperate. *Don't leave. Don't leave. Don't leave.*

"You'd think. But there's always something a little different. If nothing else, the people are different."

I didn't want to think that he really meant the *girls* were different.

I stood up abruptly and gave him what I hoped was a seductive smile. "Let's dance."

We danced fast, we danced slow. Even if the music was fast, we danced however we wanted. I loved that about Dylan. The fact that he never conformed to the expected. It was so unlike me, and I began to think that maybe it was true what they said: opposites really did attract.

He was spending the summer as a beach bum, while I was working, worrying about a budget and chores, and being responsible for the care and upkeep of my grandparents' house. Sure, when he went into the army, responsibility would be all over him. But first, he was taking a true vacation away from it.

I admired and envied him at the same time. It seemed so courageous to set out with a plan that was nothing more than seeing what the next day would bring. No lists, no tasks, no budget. To be a free spirit. To see where life took you.

It had taken him to me, and I didn't know what to do about it in the long run. To accept that these few days, these last hours would be all that we'd ever have, and make the most of them? Or shy away from the challenge?

But how could I know which choice wouldn't lead to regrets?

Maybe they both did. Maybe it was only a question of the kind of regrets—regrets for doing something, regrets for not doing it.

I was getting way too philosophical and heavy here. And maybe Dylan realized it, because he drew me close while we were dancing and began nuzzling my neck. I stopped thinking about regrets and choices and the future.

I got swept away in the now.

We stayed at the club until it closed at two. Then we walked out into the night, to the beach where the waves lapped at the shore. Since tomorrow was my legitimate day off, I wasn't worried about staying out late, because I could sleep in.

For a while anyway. Then I'd get up and make a picnic lunch and go sailing with Dylan.

He put his hands on my waist and brought me against him, dipped his head, and kissed me. Long, lazily. I loved the way he kissed.

Drawing back, he placed his forehead against mine. "Do I take you back to your place . . . or to mine?"

"For tonight, to mine."

Maybe tomorrow, after another day with him, another evening, I could give him the answer he wanted.

CHAPTER 27

Wednesday morning I basked in the luxury of sleeping in. Although I'd told Dylan that I wouldn't sleep in his tent, he hadn't been in any rush to get me home. We'd taken our time, walking along the beach, kissing, talking. It was as though once he accepted that he would be sleeping solo, he was okay with it.

Disappointed, sure. *I* would have been disappointed if he hadn't been.

But no hard feelings. Total understanding.

It had taken us more than two hours to make our way back to my place. Even then, we'd gone to the crow's nest, searched out the dolphins in the bay—using the faint lights from town, the moon, and the stars. We'd talked some more and kissed a lot more.

It was close to dawn before I crawled into bed.

So now I was waking up, stretching, grateful for a true day off. A day to spend with Dylan without the guilt of lying to my boss. Or most of the day. It was already close to noon. I had a sailboat to secure.

I got out of bed, shuffled to the desk, and powered up my computer. It was the first time in days that I'd had a chance to look at my horoscope. Almost since Dylan had come into my life. I clicked the shortcut and went straight to my horoscope.

You're not the only one thinking of the cost of commitment. A major change is on the horizon. Be prepared.

A commitment and a major change? I sat on the edge of the bed. It could only be talking about one thing: Dylan. And our relationship. We were going to bump it up to the next level.

I got up, walked into the hallway, opened the door to the bathroom—

And froze.

A strange guy was standing at the sink brushing his teeth. He gave me a frothy grin. "Hey."

"Who the hell are you?"

"Mike. Amy said I could—"

I held up my hand. "Never mind. Just hurry up, will ya? I need the bathroom."

"Oh, yeah, sure."

He spit, rinsed his toothbrush—at least, I hoped it was his, and not mine. He wiped his mouth then sidled out past me.

"This is a great—"

I slammed the door. Another stray. Another guy. The summer of girls that I'd expected to have was turning into the summer of guys.

But then I thought of Dylan, and decided that maybe it wasn't such a bad thing.

By one that afternoon Dylan hadn't shown up, and I had one of those *duh!?!* moments. Since we'd made plans to go sailing and the sailboat was at the campground, he'd probably expected me to meet him there, not have him come get me.

I wished I'd realized this long before, like before Amy and Chelsea had taken off in the car to get to work. I thought about asking Noah for a lift but he wasn't up yet—probably exhausted from his first night at work. Besides I sorta felt guilty that I'd forced him to get a job.

Get over it, Jen. You didn't force him.

Still, I decided to rely on my own means of transportation. I stuffed sandwiches, towels, and sunscreen into a backpack. I'd pick up anything else I needed at the CCR store once I got there. I put on an Astros baseball cap to shield my face from the sun. Then I got my bike out of the shed and headed out.

As I cycled along, the sun warming my legs and arms—I was wearing shorts and a tank top over my bathing suit—I thought of Dylan. Our relationship.

I'd only known him a short time, but I cared about him so much already. I loved spending time with him. And I felt a little guilty that I hadn't been as understanding as maybe I should have been when Chelsea had Noah move in with us. I might owe her an apology. I'd have to think on it some more. But later.

Right now, all I wanted was to think about Dylan. The blue of his eyes. The way his dark hair fell across his brow. The way the breeze ruffled it. His shoulders. His height. He was quite simply perfect. Nice. Fun. And a magnificent kisser.

I turned off the main road onto the road that led to the campground, my heart pumping as hard as my legs. I could just imagine him—standing beside his tent, hands on his hips, saying something about girls always being late. Then forgiving me for messing up—for not confirming how I was supposed to get to the campground—and giving me one of his long, slow kisses.

I cycled over the blacktop between the main building and the snack bar. I could see the trailer and motor home parked along the bay, the vehicles between which I could usually see Dylan's tent. Only it wasn't there. I could only see sand and beyond it water.

It had to be a mirage, the sun somehow reflecting off their tent making it seem invisible—like a Klingon cloaking device. That had to be it.

Peddling faster, I tore through the campground. Gasping, I braked at the edge of a paved campsite. I got off my bike, dropped it on the ground, and walked through the site to the beach. Maybe he'd moved his tent and it was hidden from view, behind another trailer. I got to the sand, but his tent was nowhere to be seen. Nowhere. The beach was practically empty, deserted. This was all wrong.

This was my day off. We were going sailing.

As I made my way to the marina, I think my staggering walk might have resembled the cat's yesterday morning. I was in shock, disbelief. I went inside. Mr. P was behind the counter.

He looked up. "Hi, Jennifer. Feeling better today?"

I nodded, but inside I was thinking, *I feel worse, so much worse*. I licked my dry lips. "Did Dylan work this morning?"

"No, those boys were gone before I did my early morning run."

Every day before dawn, he went through the campground, making sure no one had sneaked in without paying. Not that it would be easy for a trailer to do any sneaking.

"Did he say anything to you yesterday . . . about leaving, I mean?"

"Nope, but then, he wouldn't. We had a pretty informal arrangement."

"Okay. Thanks."

"Are you all right?"

I shook my head. "I'm not feeling as good as I thought I was."

"You go on home. Spend another day in bed. There's a summer flu going around."

I nodded. "That's probably it. I'll see you later."

I left the marina, walked back to where I'd left my bike, and stared at all the sand.

Dylan didn't say anything about leaving. But the truth was staring me in the face.

He was gone.

CHAPTER 28

I needed to talk with someone. And I couldn't talk to Chelsea. Not after she'd warned me that he was looking for a girl in every port. Not after all the fights we'd had.

So I went to the snack bar.

"Hey!" Amy yelled over the noise of the arcade, where a few sunburned kids had obviously decided to take some time away from the sun. "What are you doing here on your day off?"

When I didn't respond, but just walked up to the counter, she said, "You look awful. What's wrong?"

I felt awful, felt the stupid tears stinging my eyes. "Dylan's gone."

"Shit."

"I knew he was going to leave. I just didn't

know he was going to leave today. We had plans. We were going sailing . . . but his tent is gone."

"Maybe he just moved it. Closer to our place." Her eyes held hope, like she thought she could convince herself and me.

"Maybe." But my heart told me it was a false hope. He was gone. I just knew it.

"You gonna order or what?"

I looked down at the lobster-red face of the kid. He was probably about eight. At that moment, I hated the male species. "I'm gonna *what*." I turned my attention back to Amy. "I'll catch you later."

"Why don't you hang out at the pool?"

I shook my head. "It's my day off. I want to . . . do something special."

Special was pathetic. Special was pushing my bicycle along the water's edge and scouring the bodies coating the beach, looking for a familiar shape, listening for a familiar laugh, searching for that familiar lopsided smile. Holding onto the hope that Amy had tossed out to me, the hope that Dylan had just moved his tent up the beach instead of farther down the Texas coast.

Special was buying myself a coconut-flavored snow cone at the snow cone shack and then wondering why it was blue. Special was seeing couples hugging and kissing and remembering that I'd planned to spend my day doing exactly that.

I watched the sandpipers running over the sand, the seagulls swooping down from the sky. I watched the tide wash away sand castles and felt it washing away my hope as I got closer and closer to my end of the island without sighting Dylan.

Then I had a horrible thought: What if I sighted him with another girl? What if he hadn't moved onto another section of the coast but on to another girl?

No, we'd had something special. Not special enough to hold him, but special enough that it had meant something.

It had to have meant something. I just didn't know what.

So I sought out the special day I wanted. Special was putting the sunscreen on myself and lying on a blanket on the sand, wondering why he hadn't said good-bye. Wondering if he'd left like he did because I hadn't given him what he wanted.

Realizing that I'd done something really, really stupid.

I'd fallen in love with him.

CHAPTER 29

It was early evening before I finally found the energy or the desire to make my way home. I walked into the living room and slumped into a chair, barely noticed by Amy and Chelsea who were watching *Titanic*. It seemed that with Noah working, we'd regained feminine control of the TV and the remote.

I'd seen the movie a dozen times. I'd come in at a really bad place, watching Leonardo and Kate in the backseat of an old car, fogging up the windows, not knowing what the future held. My life was like that gigantic ship, sinking into the depths of the ocean. Or in my case, the depths of despair.

With a dog in her lap, beside her, and at her feet, Amy looked over at me. "Oh, my gosh, you are seriously sunburned."

"I know." I could feel the heat on my skin, the tightness, the slight pain. Yesterday, I'd had Dylan to constantly slather lotion on me. He'd done it like every ten to fifteen minutes, laughing while he did it, saying he needed to protect me from the sun. When really all he wanted was an excuse to touch me. As if he needed an excuse.

Today I hadn't been able to rouse the energy to put it on myself after that first application.

"Amy told me about tent guy boogying out of your life," Chelsea said.

I stared harder at the TV. "Go ahead and say it, Chels."

"Say what?"

"I told you so."

"I wouldn't do that."

But I heard in the echo of her voice that she was doing exactly that . . . a slight smugness that hurt as much as my sunburned skin.

"We're going to the Sandpiper after nine," Amy said. "When it isn't so busy. Noah said he'd treat us to an appetizer."

"And it'll give me a few minutes to see him,"

Chelsea said. "I miss him so bad. I haven't seen him since I left this morning because he has to be at work before I get home."

I heard the accusation in her voice, and it was the last straw. A guy I'd really liked had disappeared without a trace, and she was still harping about the little bit of time that she'd be without Noah.

I came up out of the chair like a zombie with a vengeance. "You know, Chels, I'm really getting tired of your constant, continual whining. The world doesn't revolve around you every second of every day. You need to grow up."

Chelsea's mouth dropped open, and Amy's eyes grew as large and round as the dog dish she'd bought and put in the kitchen. They were both looking at me like I'd turned into the Incredible Hulk.

I should have stopped there, but it was like things had been bottled up and now that I'd released a bit, the rest needed to follow.

"You think you're disappointed in how this summer is going? News flash! So am I. It was supposed to be you, Amy, and me having a great time. Suddenly we're sharing the place with a guy—and you didn't even bother to ask us how we might feel about it."

"Amy's asking guys—"

"You did it first. I've spent most of my time since we got here slapping my head and asking myself, 'What were you thinking when you suggested this?' I thought it would be fun to live on the island in a house near the beach with my best friends. So far, it's been nothing but one huge disappointment."

I knew I'd regret the outburst later. But not now. Now I was way too exhausted and hurting too much to care.

"I'm going to go take a shower." I took two steps before turning around and glaring at Amy. "Or will I find another strange guy in the bathroom?"

She slunk back into the corner of the couch. "Rent is expensive on the island, and we had the extra beds."

"We have extra floor space, too. Are you going to start lending it out?"

Oh, my God. I could actually see her calculating how many strays she could take in if she let them sleep on the floor.

"Never mind," I said wearily, not certain if I was saying never mind to Amy's tendency to take in strays or to Amy herself. Or to Chelsea or the dogs or the cat. I was tired of it all. I was tired of this great summer that I'd planned not being anything at all like I'd planned.

I trudged up the stairs to the shower. I welcomed the pain of the water hitting my sunburned skin. Because at least it distracted me from the pain stabbing my heart.

I'd not only lost a guy, but I was losing my best friends as well.

I was pitiful that first week after Dylan left. Absolutely pitiful.

No energy, no desire to interact with people. I was like a robot set on automatic.

I went to work, I registered guests, I listened as Chelsea moaned because she never ever saw Noah anymore.

I wanted to shout that I never saw Dylan either but you didn't hear me whining about it. I wanted to tell her—and Amy—that I'd made the mistake of falling in love. I wanted them to know how badly I was hurting. I needed to share that with someone.

But somehow our summer of being together had shifted into our summer of being apart—and I couldn't share anything with them. I thought about talking to Mrs. P, but she was close to my mom's age, which made her seem motherlike. And you didn't tell your mom about your broken heart. You told your best friends. Only I couldn't.

I was alone. An island on an island.

I hated it.

Then the second week after Dylan left, everything really went to hell.

CHAPTER 30

"We are *so* over!"

It was early evening. I looked up from the romance novel I was reading. That was how I was spending my nights. Reading about romance, since the reality of it had escaped me.

Amy turned her attention away from the DVD she was watching.

Chelsea was standing in the doorway to the living room with tears streaming down her face.

Alarm swept through me, and I got up out of the chair. "Chels, what's wrong?"

"We're over. Me and Noah."

"What happened?" Amy asked, coming up off the couch.

"I went to the Sandpiper, to surprise him—" She released a wail, ran across the room, and dropped onto the couch, drawing her long legs up beneath her.

The dogs howled. Amy told them to be quiet. Remarkably, they obeyed. She sat on one side of Chelsea. I crossed over to kneel in front of her.

"What happened?" I prodded.

She sniffed, blinked, and more tears rolled over onto her cheeks. "He was with another girl."

"What do you mean *with?*"

"Kissing! Okay? Kissing! His tongue stuck down her throat."

"Oh, wow," Amy said.

"That's not what I said when I saw them," Chelsea said. "What I said was R-rated."

"This doesn't make sense, Chels. He was kissing a girl at work?" I asked, needing clarification.

"They told me he was on his break, out back. So I went to find him. And he was with this sleazy girl. And it's all your fault," she told me, her eyes shooting daggers into me.

I sat back on my heels. "How do you figure that?"

"You made him get a job."

"I didn't tell him where to put his mouth."

"Oh, God, I hurt." She wrapped her arms around her middle and bent forward, her short hair nearly poking me in the eye. "I've never hurt this bad."

"You'll be okay, Chels," I said. The words seemed lame, but I knew the truth of them. Or at least it seemed like I was getting over Dylan. I only thought about him every minute of every day now, instead of every second.

"We need some serious depression intervention," Amy said. "Let's go out."

"I don't want to go out."

"Amy's right," I said. "Let's go have some fun, like we'd planned to do this summer."

"How can I have fun without Noah?"

"We had fun together before he came into your life," I reminded her.

"I could meet someone else, make him jealous."

"That'll backfire," I told her. "Let's just go out and forget about boys completely."

"Let's do it," she said with defiance ringing in her voice. "And be sure we lock all the doors."

An evil grin played over her face. "I never gave him a key."

Well, a girl can't forget about boys completely—even when she's trying. The first thing we did was deck ourselves out to kill. Short skirts, sexy tops, jewelry, makeup, the whole nine yards. We were going out on the town, and we were going out big time.

We hit a club called Surf's Up. Surfboards lined the walls. Susan and Tom were there, and a few other people we recognized from their party or ours. Everyone was happy to see us, and it made me feel like we were actually island people.

Known by name. Welcomed into the fold.

We ended up sitting on one side of the building where several tables had been shoved up against each other.

People asked where Noah was; Chelsea said he'd moved to China. They asked me about Dylan, and I said he'd moved to Antarctica. No one seemed to question anything more than that. The island life. Nothing was permanent. Things washed up onshore, washed away with the tide. Houses were built to last only until a storm tore them down.

And so we were three girls on our own for the night, looking to have a bit of fun. And the island guys were more than happy to provide it.

We danced and drank and ate. To look at Chelsea flirting with some surfer guys, no one would have realized that she'd had a boyfriend that morning. She was all over them, and they were all over her.

Me . . . I was still pathetic. Comparing every guy to Dylan and finding them all lacking. Their eyes were the wrong color. Their smiles too perfect.

I wanted them to make me forget about Dylan. And all they seemed to do was remind me that he was gone.

"You're hooked up with someone, aren't you?"

Sitting at the table, I looked at the guy who had dropped into the chair beside mine. He grabbed a peanut from a metal bucket and went about cracking it open, dropping the shell on the floor. A lot of peanuts had been opened around here.

He was cute—gerbil cute—with puffy cheeks and twinkling eyes. He looked like he could be fun. So why was I irritated that he'd interrupted me—when I wasn't doing anything?

"No," I said. That's all. Nothing to lead him on, nothing to extend the conversation.

"You're the one living in the last house on the island."

"Yep."

He furrowed his brow, which lifted his cheeks and made it look like he was squinting. "I saw you with a guy—tall, dark hair—"

"We're over."

"So where is he?"

"I don't know. I don't care." The lies were flying out of my mouth like bats out of cave at twilight.

He shelled another peanut, popped the nut into his mouth, and chewed. Like a cow in the pasture. His gaze never straying from me. He swallowed. "It's just that I thought the two of you looked serious."

"You thought wrong."

"Okay. So you want to dance?"

I smiled brightly. "Yes." Anything. Anywhere.

Anytime. Just take me away from here.

His name was Randy. He owned a surfboard stand on the sand. A shack, really. But the rent was cheap. And he could take in the rays all day while renting people surfboards. And in the evenings, when he closed up shop, he surfed. He'd surfed during the last hurricane.

"It was totally awesome," he said. "Huge waves."

He was so proud of what he'd done, and all I could think was: Could you get any more stupid?

"You could have been killed."

He nodded. "Yep. But it would have been worth it. It was a rush."

I was beginning to feel like the dullest girl on the planet. Maybe that's why Dylan had taken off instead of spending my day off with me. Because when it came right down to it, he was going to go play Rambo, and I was the type of person who would head to the mainland as soon as a hurricane started coming my way.

When the song ended, I went back to the table and sat down. Randy went off to get us something to drink.

Chelsea sat down beside me. "Are we having fun yet?"

"Not really."

"What are we doing here, Jen?"

"I don't know."

"I miss Noah."

"You have to forget him, Chels. He's not good enough for you. Not if he was making out with another girl."

"Maybe he wasn't. Maybe he was . . . I don't know, maybe she washed up onshore, and he was giving her mouth to mouth—"

"I thought they were behind the restaurant."

"A really high tide could have carried her to the restaurant."

I gave her a hard stare. She sighed. "I know. I'm pathetic."

"Been there, done that."

"Let's find Amy and blow this place."

So we did just that.

The three of us. Alone on the beach, walking where the water met the sand. A little tipsy from sneaking drinks when the waitress wasn't looking.

But it was wonderful, the way I'd expected

the summer to be. Me and my girlfriends. Just us. No guys. No worries. No troubles.

"Who was the chipmunk?" Amy asked.

I laughed. I'd thought of him as a gerbil. "Randy. He owns a surfboard shop."

"You're a guy magnet."

"Yeah, right. Both of you had plenty of guys hanging off you."

"Thought that's the reason we came out," Chelsea said. "To get lost in lust."

"It wasn't working."

"Whatever."

"So what are we going to do for the rest of the summer?" Amy asked.

"Work, play, have fun. Party, here and there."

"Do you know what I'm craving?" Chelsea asked. "Chocolate ice cream. Let's stop and get a tub and rent a movie."

"Let's do."

"We'll sit on the couch, eating right out of the tub. Until it's gone."

That's what I wanted. A summer of just the three of us. So why did it suddenly seem so unappealing? Why did I want more?

Why did I want Dylan?

CHAPTER 31

We sat on the couch in the dark with a movie playing and strawberry candles burning on the coffee table. Not romantic. Just peaceful. I was sitting in the middle, holding the tub of ice cream while we all dipped into it, scooped out some, and ate it.

"This is so good," Chelsea said. "It almost makes me forget about Noah. Almost."

We'd actually gone three minutes without her mentioning him.

"He'll be getting off work soon. I guess he'll spend the night with that slut he was kissing."

"Does it really matter, Chelsea?"

"Yeah, it matters. It hurts to think about it. Don't you ever think about Dylan?"

I felt tears sting my eyes. "He's been gone

two weeks, and this is the first time that you've asked how I feel."

"I just figured if you were feeling bad, you'd let us know."

"When? When you're with Noah?"

She shifted around on the couch until she was facing me. "Did he hurt you?"

"He just left without saying good-bye. We were supposed to spend the day together. And he was gone. What do you think the answer to that question is?"

We heard a door downstairs open.

Chelsea inhaled a deep breath. "Didn't you lock the door?"

"Yeah."

"Then how did Noah get in?"

"It's probably Alex," Amy said calmly, dipping ice cream out of the carton. "I gave him a key."

I stared at her. "You gave him a key?"

"Yeah. In case we weren't here, and he needed to get in."

"What about Mike?"

"No, I didn't give him a key. Besides, in case you haven't noticed, he's not around anymore."

I hadn't noticed.

Alex walked into the living room and grinned. Here was something else that I hadn't noticed. He was cute. I'd never thought of red hair and freckles as cute, but on him they were.

"Hey, babe," he said.

Babe?

"Hi," Amy said.

He sauntered over, put his hand on the back of the couch, leaned down, and kissed her.

Kissed her.

When he pulled away, she held up her ice cream–laden spoon and he took a bite.

"How was work?" she asked.

"Busy." He yawned. "I'm gonna shower and go to bed." He winked. "Wake me when you come to bed."

"Okay."

I watched him walk out of the room. Then I looked at Chelsea. Her jaw was hanging down. So was mine.

I looked back at Amy. "What was that about?"

Shrugging, she took a bite of ice cream.

"You have a boyfriend," Chelsea said with a sort of awe.

Amy grinned and nodded.

"When did this happen?" I asked.

"I don't know. One night we were in the crow's nest, just talking, and we talked all night. Chelsea was busy with Noah . . . and you wanted to be alone after Dylan left . . . and I was lonely and there was Alex. Always willing to talk, to be there. And I like him."

"You have a boyfriend," Chelsea said again.

"Yeah, it's kinda neat."

"You never said anything," I said. "Whenever we drove to work . . . you could have said something then."

"I didn't want you to feel bad. I knew you were upset about Dylan. And Chelsea only wants to talk about Noah."

"That's not true," Chelsea said.

"Yes, it is. It was supposed to be *our* summer, but I was alone."

"You should have said something," I said. "You should have made us realize—"

"That's the thing, Jen. I shouldn't have had to say anything. Why do you think I invited stray guys to stay here? Why do you think I gather stray animals around me? Because we're friends, but I'm always on the outside of the circle."

"That's not true."

"Yes, it is, but it doesn't bother me. I love you. I love Chelsea. You two are the best. But I've never been as important to you as you are to me. And now I have Alex." She stood up. "'Night, guys."

I stared after her, then turned to Chelsea.

"I feel like a total jerk. Do we ignore her?"

"I didn't think so," Chelsea said slowly. "But she has a boyfriend. And I had no idea."

I set the tub of ice cream on the coffee table, scooted to the end of the couch, brought my feet up, and wrapped my arms around my legs.

"I can't believe that all these years Amy hasn't felt like she was inside our circle."

"I know. Maybe it's PMS."

"Yeah, right," I said.

But it wasn't. And I knew it wasn't. I ran my fingers through my hair.

"I always thought I was such a good friend to you and to Amy. But I've made your life miserable, and now Amy . . . she has a boyfriend and I had absolutely no idea."

"Amy has a boyfriend and we don't. That sucks big time," Chelsea said.

I laughed. It was so typical of her. Here I was soul searching, and she was looking at it from the personal perspective of not having a boyfriend.

"What's so funny?" Chelsea asked.

"This summer. The way it's going. Nothing like I'd planned."

"Maybe that's the problem. You plan too much. You should just let things happen."

"I don't plan too much. I just like to know—" I stopped. I was so tired of arguing with her about every little thing.

"I'm glad Amy has a boyfriend," I said instead. "Good for her. She deserves one."

"What do you know about this guy?"

I shook my head, embarrassed to have to admit, "Nothing."

A banging on the door downstairs had us both shooting off the couch.

"Chelsea! Open up!"

"No way, jerk," she said with a hiss. She ran

out of the living room to the stairs and shouted. "Go away, you jerk!"

"Come on, Chels! I can explain!"

I stood in the living room doorway. I could see her wavering. "Don't do it, Chels. Don't give in. Think about him in that lip-lock."

"You were kissing another girl!" she yelled.

"But I love you!"

I could see tears forming in her eyes.

"He wouldn't have been kissing her if he really loved you," I said.

"Oh, shut up," she said, like it was all my fault—again. "Don't you think I know that?"

She stomped past me and into her bedroom. I followed right behind her.

"What are you going to do?" I asked.

"Throw his things off the balcony."

She started gathering up his clothes, tossing them onto the bed into a pile.

"I'll show him, I'll—" She released a blood-curdling scream.

I snapped my head around to look where she was looking—at the balcony door. Noah was pressed up against it.

"Come on, babe, let me explain."

Chelsea glared at me accusingly. "I thought you said only Spider-Man could climb onto the balcony."

"I guess if he backed his truck up, climbed in the bed of it, it would give him enough height—"

"It doesn't matter. He's here. What do I do now?"

He was still yelling her name. Over and over. Begging her to understand.

"Stay strong," I urged her.

She nodded and gritted her teeth. "I will. But how do I throw his things out?"

"I'll grab a pile, run downstairs, and toss them out the door."

"You'd do that?"

"What are best friends for?"

I took an armload of his clothes and dashed out of her room, down the stairs. I opened the door, tossed his clothes onto the ground. And there was his truck. The bed right beneath the balcony giving him a way to reach the balcony and climb on.

I quickly closed the door, locked it, and headed back upstairs. I staggered to a stop just inside the door to Chelsea's room. She and Noah were on the bed, wrapped around each other. In between kisses, she was crying and blubbering, he was apologizing and explaining.

I shouldn't have left her alone. I shouldn't have gone downstairs to toss out his clothes. I should have gone onto the balcony and tossed him off, onto his butt. I should have known her well enough to know that she had no willpower. He'd break through her resolve.

She'd given in without a fight. I would at least make the guy crawl over broken glass, beg—right before turning my back on him and walking away.

No way would his mouth even get close to mine again. Chelsea was pathetic, absolutely pathetic, wanting a boyfriend so badly that she'd forgive him for anything.

I stepped out of the room and quietly closed the door. The ice cream had leaked through the carton, onto the coffee table, onto the floor. The dogs were licking it off the floor, the cat had leaped onto the table and was going at it there.

I should have chased them away and cleaned

it up properly. But the truth was I didn't care anymore.

Not about Chelsea and Noah or Amy and Alex or me and Dylan. Only there wasn't a me and Dylan.

I went up the stairs and into my bedroom. I didn't bother to turn on the lights. Just crawled into my bed, lay in the dark, and let the tears fall. And faced the truth.

Unlike Noah, Dylan hadn't come back. Unlike Chelsea, I wouldn't have taken him back . . . even if he'd given me the chance.

CHAPTER 32

"I quit."

It was early morning, a week after the Noah-caught-in-a-lip-lock scare. Amy and I were sitting on the floor beside the coffee table in the living room cutting out coupons and making our list for our trek to the grocery store so we could go right after work. We were still following our budget pretty closely, and so far, we'd had no problem covering our bills.

Amy and I looked over at Chelsea. She was always the last to get up. We were usually yelling at her that we needed to go. But this morning she was standing in the doorway . . . well, the only way to describe her stance was . . . *defiant*.

"You quit what?" I asked. *Being with Noah? Not after what I'd witnessed lately.*

"I quit my job at the campground."

I released a brittle laugh. "You can't quit."

"I can and I did. Just now. I borrowed Noah's truck and drove out there and told Mrs. Plackette I wouldn't be coming back."

I stared at her, unable to believe this. "How are you going to pay for your share of the bills?"

I hated to admit it, but I liked having Noah and Alex around, dividing our expenses by five instead of three—now that they were contributing. It gave us some play-around money. Not that I was doing any real playing, but still. I was able to relax a little. I didn't want to lose that.

"I got a job at the Sandpiper, working nights. So Noah and I can be together during the day. And we'll be together at night."

"I got you that job at the campground."

"Yeah, and I hate it. I hate not being with Noah."

"You owe the campground—"

"I don't owe them anything, Jen."

"We'll be shorthanded, it'll make the work harder on everyone else."

"They can hire someone else."

"Everyone already has summer jobs."

"Not my problem."

"I can't believe you're doing this to us."

"I'm not doing anything to you. You think the world revolves around *you*. And it doesn't."

I looked over at Amy. "Say something."

"What's to say? She quit already. It's done."

There was something strange about the way she was looking at me, then Chelsea.

"You knew she was going to quit," I said.

"Chelsea told me she was thinking about it."

What was going on here? There was a time when my friends and I had shared everything. Now I felt like there were secrets and things going on behind my back.

"Are you going to quit?"

"No. But I'm going to ask if I can work in the store. I'm tired of smelling like boiling hot dogs all the time."

I turned my attention back to Chelsea. "This was supposed to be the summer of us."

"It still is."

"No, it's not. It's the summer of you and Noah, the summer of Amy and her strays. The summer of . . . " I couldn't say it. The summer of me. Alone. The island.

"Never mind. Do what you think is right."

"I already have."

And with that she walked into her bedroom and slammed the door.

Amy was quiet as she drove us to work. I looked out the passenger window and watched the island go past me. The shacks, the dunes, the sandpipers. The people sunbathing, playing in the surf.

"I can't believe Chelsea is running her life totally around Noah," I said distractedly.

"She's insecure."

I snapped my head around and looked at Amy. "Huh?"

She cast a quick glance my way. "She's insecure. He was kissing another girl. She's worried about losing him."

"I think he would be worth losing."

"Love is strange. It has no rhyme or reason. It simply is."

"Who are you now? Buddha?"

She smiled. "No. I just understand it—as much as anyone can understand it, I guess."

I shifted around in the seat. "I'm so sorry,

Amy. I'm sorry that I haven't paid more attention to what was going on in your life, to the fact that you have a boyfriend—"

She waved her hand. "No big deal. You were all wrapped up in Dylan."

"Just for a few days. The rest of the time . . . I should have noticed what was going on with you."

"It doesn't matter, Jen."

But it did matter. It mattered that all of us were falling in and out of love this summer and we weren't sharing the experiences with each other. We were drifting apart.

"Do you love Alex?"

She nodded, a secretive smile playing over her face.

"This is a stupid question, because he lives in the house with us, and I should know, but he's so quiet. What's he like? Really?"

"He's a deep thinker. Supersmart. And we so get each other. We don't have to talk unless we want to. It's amazing, Jen."

She pulled onto the road that led into the campground. Then she parked the car and looked over at me.

"I was jealous when you were with Dylan. You had a guy, Chelsea had a guy. I had a dog." Tears filled her eyes. "I was glad when Dylan just packed up and left. I'm sorry, Jen. I didn't want to be there for you. And I wasn't."

"I haven't been there for you."

"Did you like him a lot?"

What could I say? She was asking, but I didn't feel like telling her the truth. "No, I just liked him a little." I looked toward the beach where his tent used to be. I did that every time we came to the campground, like I thought one day I'd look out and his tent would miraculously be there again.

"I'm sorry, Jen."

I took a deep breath. "Nothing to be sorry for, except for the fact that you're going to be freezing your butt off today. Come on, let's get to work."

June 22 came and went. Amy and Chelsea didn't switch bedrooms. Big surprise there. Amy and Alex liked the room they were in. It had memories. Chelsea and Noah were still making up and needed the big bedroom to do that.

The truth was, I figured they both thought it was more trouble than it was worth to move all their stuff. But come July 22, I was taking over that room.

It would be the turning point of my summer. I absolutely knew it.

Because except for the little time I'd spent with Dylan, my summer sucked so far. Big time.

Amy and I hardly ever saw Chelsea. She and Noah were practically superglued together. Work, play . . . whatever, they never left each other's sight. I wasn't sure that was the best way to handle a relationship, but I'd decided that it wasn't really any of my business.

Who would have thought when I'd had this brilliant idea for a summer together that a month into it, I would have accepted that *together* was not where we were anymore.

Amy and I spent time together. Working at the campground, basking in the late afternoon sun after work. We'd watch a movie in the evenings. Then Alex would return from working at some bar where he was the bartender. He always came through the doorway with a

"Hey, babe," and a smile that said he thought she was the best. And then they'd disappear.

And I'd be alone. I avoided my once favorite place—the crow's nest—because the memories of my time there with Dylan always overwhelmed me. So I'd sit on the balcony, watch the night and the stars, the lights of the ships on the water. It was romantic and sad at the same time. Then I'd hear Chelsea and Noah return from work and go into their bedroom.

I'd hear them talking, giggling, moaning, and I'd get up and go to my room. Lie in my bed in the dark, and think about a guy who I'd never see again. It was pathetic. It was like I was going through the stages of grief or something.

Then one morning I woke up to a horoscope that read:

Hug a best friend. It'll improve your outlook.

And it changed everything.

CHAPTER 33

"What was *that* for?" Amy asked.

She'd been coming out of the bathroom as I was heading to the kitchen.

"Just doing what my horoscope advised and hugging a best friend. It's supposed to improve my outlook."

"Did it?"

I took a deep breath, thought about it . . . "Not really."

"Bummer. I was hoping you might do me a favor tonight."

"Just because my outlook on life sucks doesn't mean I won't do you a favor. Just ask."

"Will you watch the dogs?"

Okay, that was asking me to do something above and beyond. I stared at her. "Huh?"

"Noah and Chelsea are working—like always. Alex isn't."

"Then let him watch them."

"Well, that's the thing. We've never really had a chance to have a real date. Tonight we thought we'd go to the mainland, catch a movie, or whatever."

I so did not want to do this.

"The dogs are your responsibility. And Noah's. I never wanted anything to do with them."

"But if I leave them in my room, and they need to go out, they'll make a mess. All you have to do is walk them. Come on, Jen. What have I ever asked for?"

"Let's see." I ticked off on my fingers. "A little dog, a medium-size dog, a big dog, and a cat. Oh, yeah. And a boyfriend."

"The boyfriend you don't mind because he helps with the expenses."

I nodded. "Okay. I don't mind the boyfriend."

"You wouldn't mind the dogs either if you got to know them. Please, Jen. I won't be able to have fun if I'm worried about them."

I sighed. It wasn't like I had any exciting plans for the night—except to curl up with a new romance novel. "Oh, all right."

She beamed her brightest smile. "Thanks!"

I walked back toward my room.

"Where are you going?" she asked.

"To get ready for work. I've lost my appetite for breakfast."

"You guys are pathetic, you know that?"

We were in the utility room, and I was trying to get leashes put on each of the dogs. I tried to remember what Amy had named the two newest dogs and couldn't. So out of fairness, I renamed Tiny so the dogs became Dog 1, Dog 2, and Dog 3. From smallest to largest.

Dog 1 was yipping, Dog 2 kept leaping on me every time I got close to having the leash attached to its collar, and Dog 3 was throwing itself against the door.

"Okay, already, I know you need to go. Just hold on."

I finally got all the leashes snapped into place. I held tightly to my end. Then I made the mistake of opening the door. They bounded out like steak heaven was waiting on the other side.

And I went with them.

"Hold on!"

I held tight to the leashes while closing the door. I locked it and slipped the keys into my shorts pocket. "Okay, fellas, let's go."

And they did, pulling me along while they sniffed the ground. Our journey was a series of quick walks, then standing around waiting for one or more of them to mark its territory. We headed up the road toward the beach. My goal was to walk them until they were worn out and pee'd-out. I didn't want to have to go through this again.

We walked past the Coast Guard station. A Coastie waved and yelled, "Beautiful dogs!"

Was he kidding? I guess they weren't as ugly as I'd thought. As a matter of fact, they were looking better than they had when Amy first took them in.

"Thanks!" I yelled back.

Then I looked at the dogs. "Amy takes good care of you, doesn't she?"

She'd also looked spectacular earlier when she and Alex left. She'd gone all out, putting on a halter dress and actually styling her hair. The normally straight brown strands had been curling over her shoulders. And her makeup had been perfect. Alex was one lucky guy.

The dogs and I made our way over the dunes. I had a feeling that my shoulder was going to be aching in the morning. It was aching now. How did Amy do this every night?

Then the dogs went wild, bounding over the sand, headed for the surf, jerking me along. I figured once they got to the water, they'd retreat. But nooo!

In they went, bounding over the waves, splashing, jumping on me. I started laughing. This was insane!

Then Dog 3 knocked me down. I screeched and hit the water, the sand. Laughing harder. For no reason, except that it felt good.

I flopped back, letting the water rush over me and retreat.

"Come here, you!" I grabbed Dog 3, holding him close.

And it suddenly occurred to me that I was hugging man's best friend. *A best friend.* Just like my horoscope had advised.

And it did improve my outlook on life!

The dogs licked my cheeks, my neck, my hands. I buried my face in Dog 3's fur. Why was I spending my summer moping around? I lifted my head. Remarkably, the dogs had calmed.

We sat there, at the water's edge, and watched the sun go down. And I made a decision. It was time that I took charge of my life again.

"Let's have a huge Fourth of July bash," I announced after everyone got home that night. "We have a week to plan. They're going to have fireworks at the campground. We could have fireworks here—"

"Isn't there some sort of ordinance against fireworks on individual property?" Alex asked.

"That'll be your job to get it okayed."

He nodded. "All right."

"It'll be great, guys. We'll invite everyone we know on the island. It'll be even bigger and better than the last party we had here."

"Sounds cool," Noah said.

"Because it'll *be* cool," I assured him.

He yawned. "Just leave me a note with instructions. I'm wiped out from work. I'm going to bed."

Chelsea started to go with him, then stopped and faced me. "I'm not too tired yet. Let's get this thing planned."

Alex went to bed as well, but Amy, Chelsea, and I sat on the floor around the coffee table.

Before we got started, I looked at Amy and asked, "How was your date?"

She blushed. "We had such a good time. How did it go here?"

I had my hand buried in Dog 3's fur, his head in my lap, his doleful eyes looking up at me. I smiled. "We did okay."

Then we started discussing our plans: decorations, food, drinks. How we were going to afford it all.

We decided people would bring their own drinks and whatever they wanted to go on the grill. We'd provide lots of chocolate desserts and the space. And I'd be cool with people in the house. We'd invite the island people that we knew. Some people from the campground—if Amy and I agreed that they were cool enough.

We'd have an open invite policy. Anyone could bring anyone.

The object was to get lost in the crowd, to have a super great time.

I had a mission now, a purpose. And I was really excited about it. I thought about the party constantly. Amy and I talked about it on the way to work and on the way home. It was going to be the absolute best.

I had everything planned out perfectly.

There was just one thing I hadn't planned on happening.

But then no one else had, either.

CHAPTER 34

Tonight Cupid will have you within his sights—retreat if you don't like the prospects!

Retreat? No way! I was ready for a little romance, because I was totally over Dylan and ready to move on to new conquests.

July Fourth was hot almost beyond endurance, but it didn't really seem to matter. There was a breeze blowing across the ocean, across the island. There was excitement in the air that I couldn't explain.

Party atmosphere. Amy and I both felt it, even before we left work.

The partying was scheduled to begin as the sun began to set, but with island time, it started when anyone, everyone wanted.

Alex had taken the night off from work, and

he became our official bartender. Chelsea and Noah—to everyone's complete surprise!—called in sick. Like their boss wasn't going to figure that one out.

But it was something for them to worry about—not me.

I'd adopted the new attitude that nothing was my problem . . . unless it really was my problem. I couldn't run the lives of my friends. I had to let them make their own choices, just like I had to make mine. And for tonight my choice was to have the best time of my life, to drink and dance, and find a guy who would take my mind completely off Dylan.

And there were ample selections to choose from. Many of them cute, a couple of them very charming—but most important, they were all here. Available. Not about to take off for parts unknown.

"Alex made some margaritas," Amy said when I walked into the kitchen to check on the brownies that I'd put into the oven earlier.

"Sounds good," I said.

"Can you believe how many people are here already?" she asked.

"Must be at least fifty."

"Where did they all come from?"

"Here, there, everywhere."

I took the brownies out of the oven.

"You're okay with people inside the house?" she asked.

"Sure. It's a new me, Amy. Live and let live. I'm an islander. Take life easy."

"I'm glad we decided to spend the summer here," she said. "You had a great idea."

"Yeah, it's been good." I leaned near her and winked. "And you got a boyfriend."

"He's thinking of moving to College Station at the end of the summer, to be near me. He says college towns always need bartenders."

"You really like him," I mused.

She nodded enthusiastically. "A lot."

I hugged her. I didn't know why. Maybe I wanted some of her true happiness to rub off on me, because the truth was, if I was honest with myself, I was only pretending to be happy, and I was afraid that it showed.

There was a time when I wouldn't have pretended with my friends. I would have told them that I'd never been so lonely in my entire life, that the loneliness was like a sharp pain in my heart that pricked every time I moved. But they were happy, and I didn't want to bring them down. Not any more. Not for the rest of the summer.

I went into the living room, and Alex poured me a strawberry margarita. He grinned at me. "This was a great idea. We can drink till we drop, and no one has to drive."

"Exactly." I took a sip of the thick frozen concoction. It was good. "You know, if you hurt Amy I'll break your kneecaps."

He laughed, apparently taking no offense at my statement. "Then my kneecaps are safe. I'd never hurt her. I like her too much."

"Good."

I made my way outside. Someone had set the stereo speakers on the balcony, and music was raining down on us. Chelsea and Noah were manning the grill. The aroma of charred meat wafted through the air.

"Steaks?" I asked incredulously once I got near enough to see what he was cooking.

"We thought we should go all out, and we got a huge discount from the guy who supplies the restaurant," Chelsea said.

"My Chels is a bargain shopper," Noah said.

Chelsea stepped away from him, took my arm, and led me a short distance away. "You and I haven't really had a chance to talk since I quit the campground. So you see how it was with me and Noah? We just never saw each other."

I wanted to say that explanation gave him no excuse for kissing another girl, but I bit my tongue. Chelsea had to live with her choices, not me. "Yeah, I see."

Although I really didn't.

"He wasn't kissing that girl. She was kissing him. She'd gotten drunk—"

"Chels, it's not my business."

"I just don't want you thinking badly of him."

"As long as you're happy, that's all that matters."

"I am happy, Jen. Totally."

"Then I'm happy, too."

And I was. For Chelsea and for Amy. And in a way for myself. Because I was free to play the field. And I planned to do exactly that. I was going to have fun with every guy here, dance until my feet ached, drink until my head spun, eat until my stomach hurt. Then I was going to watch the fireworks at this end of the island, climb into the crow's nest and watch them going off at the other end of the island, near the campground.

And I didn't plan to watch them alone.

Chelsea had gone totally still and quiet. I figured she was ready to get back to Noah.

"You and Noah have fun. I'll catch up with you later. Right now, according to my horoscope, I have a guy to hook up with."

I had no idea who he might be, but I had to believe that he was out there somewhere, lost in the crowd, waiting for me to find him.

I turned around, and my brain stopped functioning. My heart hammered, but nothing else worked. My legs wouldn't move, my lungs wouldn't draw in air. I simply stood there like a dolt.

I'd planned tonight to perfection. Planned every minute. Every aspect.

But I hadn't planned for Dylan to return.

If at all possible, he looked more gorgeous. More tan. His black hair longer, shaggy looking.

He needed to shave. I curled my fingers against my palm to stop myself from reaching up and touching the roughness of his face, from reaching out for him period.

In thirty-five days—not that I'd been counting the days since he left—I'd changed. And he probably had as well. I wasn't going to be pathetic like Chelsea. I wasn't going to let him sweep me into his arms.

I was going to be cool, calm, collected. I was going to walk away as though he was nothing. As though he didn't make my heart sing. As though the very sight of him didn't cause pleasure to ripple through me.

I wasn't even going to acknowledge him. I was simply going to turn and take a step away and then another and another until I couldn't see him, smell him, hear his breathing. Until he was a speck of dust, a forgotten memory, a—

"I missed our sailing date," he said quietly.

I gave him a jerky nod, swallowing hard. Then to my eternal mortification and embarrassment, I burst into tears.

CHAPTER 35

"You *what*?!" Chelsea asked.

I was in my bedroom, wiping my eyes, trying to regain my composure after making a mad dash into the house. So much for remaining calm and cool. I'd run off like a total lunatic.

Chelsea had followed close on my heels. Noah had actually blocked Dylan from following me. His protective stance just made me cry harder. I'd been so unfair to him all summer. Once inside, Chelsea had yelled, "Emergency, Amy!"

And Amy had stopped whatever she was doing.

Now they were both sitting on my bed, holding me, comforting me. Being there like they hadn't been all summer. Or maybe they had been, and I just hadn't noticed.

I sniffed, wiped my eyes, and rasped, "I fell in love with him."

"Why didn't you tell us?" Amy asked.

"What could you have done about it?"

"Been a little more sympathetic?"

"Bought lots of chocolate ice cream!" Chelsea said. "We could have been there for you."

"I felt so stupid. You warned me that he wouldn't stay. I knew he wouldn't stay—"

"But your heart isn't your brain," Amy said. "You can't control it."

I started crying again. Not just because Dylan had shown up, but for everything.

"I didn't know y'all anymore," I confessed. "We had no harmony. We each had our own problems, troubles . . . we didn't seem to care about each other anymore."

"We always cared," Chelsea said. "Maybe we got bad about showing it, but we always cared."

"What are you going to do now that he's back?" Amy asked.

"I don't know. My first thought was this enormous gladness because he was here . . . and then I thought what a pathetic loser I was. To be so glad when he'd hurt me so much. He didn't even say good-bye."

"Did you think I was pathetic when I got back together with Noah after he kissed that slut?" Chelsea asked.

I was embarrassed to admit it, but I was ready for honesty between us again. "Yeah, I did."

"I love him, Jen. He's not perfect, and the truth is, sometimes guys are totally stupid." She shrugged. "But he came back."

"I know that Noah came back—"

"Not Noah." She laughed lightly, the kind of laugh that we used to share when one of us was being silly, and we thought it was funny but didn't want the person to feel like an idiot. "Dylan. Dylan came back."

"So what do I do about it?"

"What do you want to do about it?"

I shook my head, majorly embarrassed.

"Tell us, Jen," Amy urged.

I bit my lip and took a deep breath. "I lay here every night in the dark, alone, wishing he'd climb onto the balcony like Noah had—I thought that was so desperately romantic, Chels. I think it made me a little jealous that night—that he'd risked his neck like that. And I wished Dylan would come into the house, and up the stairs, and open the door to my room and smile at me the way Alex smiles at you, Amy. When Alex smiles at you, it's like his whole face lights up, like you are the most important thing in his life. And he doesn't want to be anywhere else, except with you. And that made me jealous, too.

"And maybe that's why I couldn't tell you guys the truth about Dylan. Because you had what I wanted . . . and when I'd had it, I couldn't hold onto it. And this summer wasn't supposed to be about us falling in love, or having crushes, or broken hearts. It was about us saying good-bye to each other."

Chelsea hugged me tightly. "Oh, Jen, we're never going to say good-bye to each other. Don't you get it? We're friends for life. And it doesn't matter if we're sleeping in the same house or sleeping hundreds of miles apart—we'll always be there for each other. No matter what."

"Exactly," Amy said. "So you want me and Chels to go beat up Dylan?"

Laughing, I shook my head. These were my best friends. My very best friends. I'd lost sight of that for a while. I wasn't going to lose sight of it again.

"No, I don't want you to beat him up. I know I planned this party, but will you understand if I don't hang around?"

"Depends on where you're going," Chelsea said.

"I'm going sailing."

Dylan and I didn't talk. I didn't want to talk. I wanted to be with him, I couldn't deny that. And I wanted to talk to him eventually. Just not at first. Because I didn't know what to say, and I was afraid if we started talking, I'd start crying again. I'd find myself in his arms, his mouth on mine—just like Chelsea and Noah that night he climbed onto the balcony. I wanted to be a bit stronger than Chelsea. I wanted Dylan to crawl a little.

Okay. I wanted him to crawl a lot. It was a delicate balance, because I wanted him to crawl, but not so much that he left again.

I thought about all this as I sat on the back of his motorcycle, hugging him, trying to convince myself that I didn't like the strength I felt in him as we traveled over the road toward the campground. He was so fit, so warm, so sturdy.

I had my face pressed to his back. I could smell his spicy soap, and I wondered if he was camped at the campground, if he'd arrived after I left work. I wondered if Zach was here as well, visiting whatever island girl he'd hooked up with when they were here before.

An awful thought struck me like a bolt from the sky. What if Dylan was here not because of me as I'd hoped, but because of Zach? Because Zach was missing someone?

I had a hundred questions but only one that needed answering. The rest were just a delay tactic, a way to postpone getting to the heart of the matter—which was exactly that. Our hearts.

He parked on the asphalt. I climbed off the bike and handed him his helmet.

"Jennifer—"

"Let's get to the sailboat. I called. Mr. Plackette will have it ready for us. It'll be dark soon. I'd like to be on the lagoon when the fireworks go off."

"Okay."

He loosened the restraints on a backpack that was tied to the back of his bike and carried it with him. I led the way toward the dock where lights glittered pale in the waning light of day. The sailboat was there, tied to the dock, bobbing in the water. It was small, nothing fancy. Room enough for two.

I sat on the edge of the dock, then lowered myself into the boat. "Get in, and then untie it."

Dylan did as I ordered. He moved to the middle of the boat.

"We'll use the paddles to get us out into the lagoon. Then we'll hoist the sail," I said.

"You sound like a sailor."

"A fake sailor. I don't know all the terminology. I just know how to get the sails up, how to catch the wind, and guide the boat."

"Okay."

We were as quiet making our way out into the center of the lagoon as we'd been on the motorcycle, but here I was more aware of the silence stretching between us. When we were far enough out, I raised the sail, watched the wind billow the cloth, took hold of the rudder, and steered us around the lagoon.

Occasionally a motor boat passed by us, on its way back to shore. But for the most part, it was just the two of us on the smooth water between the island and the mainland.

"Are we ever going to talk?" he asked, his voice low, as though he was hesitant to disturb the hush of night falling.

The sun was setting, night easing in, and I felt safe. If I started crying, he'd never see the tears now.

"You just left without a word. Now you show up, and you think everything is going to be okay?"

"I know it's not okay."

"We had plans to spend the day together."

"I know that. I was scared, Jennifer."

I looked at him then, really looked at him. He was sitting in the center of the boat, bent over slightly, his elbows planted on his thighs, his gaze on me.

"Of what? Of going into the army?"

"Of you. Of what I was feeling."

My heart thudded against my chest. "What were you feeling?"

"I was falling for you. Hard. I didn't want that. I had these plans, I'd been making them for two years. I wanted to camp all along the coast. I wanted to meet girls—"

"Did you?" I asked, hating the hurt that echoed in my voice. "Did you meet girls?"

"I met some, but I didn't get close to them. I kissed a couple. But I compared everyone to you. And I lay awake every night thinking about you, wishing I was with you. Can you stop this boat?"

"Yeah, we just have to take down the sail."

We did. Then we were in the middle of the lagoon, the boat bobbing gently on the water, staring at each other, not talking.

"Dylan—"

"Jenni—"

We both released a nervous laugh.

"You first," I said.

"No, you go ahead."

"Just talk to me."

"I brought you something."

He grabbed his backpack, unzipped it,

reached inside, pulled out a wooden box, and handed it to me. It was beautiful. Dark wood. Dolphins carved on the lid.

"Look inside," he said, his voice low.

I raised the hinged lid. The box was filled with sand dollars. Perfect, white, complete sand dollars.

Tears stinging my eyes, I lifted my gaze to his.

"I couldn't stop thinking about you," he said. "I tried, I really did. Zach would want to go to the beach to meet girls. I'd go, and then I'd start searching for a sand dollar. And every time I found one, I'd think of your smile or how confident you were when you thought you'd beat me at pool or the smell of chocolate chip cookies in your hair."

He took the box from me, set it aside, and wrapped his hands around mine. His were trembling slightly. He'd said he was scared back when he first left. Was he scared now, too?

"I think I fell in love with you, Jennifer."

Joy surged through me. This was better than him climbing onto the balcony.

"That wasn't supposed to happen," he

continued. He released what sounded like a nervous, self-conscious laugh. "This was supposed to be my summer of girls. Flings. One-nighters. I don't know. And then I met you and I wasn't thinking about my fantasies anymore. You were my fantasy."

"Only I wouldn't sleep with you."

He shook his head. "It wasn't that. You would have eventually."

"Ha! A lot you know!"

"Tell me you weren't thinking about it. That last night. You almost came back to the tent with me."

"I would have hated you so much if I had and then you'd left—"

"I wouldn't have left. Which is the reason I left." He groaned. "It's so hard to explain. I knew if I stayed any longer, if I had another day with you that I wouldn't want to leave with Zach. All my careful planning would have been for nothing."

I thought of the party I'd planned, the summer I'd planned. "Maybe when we make our plans, we need to allow for the unexpected."

"Then things wouldn't be planned, would they?"

"Where is Zach now?"

"Last I saw him, he was on his way down to Padre Island." In the encroaching night, I could see his familiar smile, one corner of his mouth hitching up. "With our tent."

"Where have you been sleeping?"

"I have a sleeping bag." He shook his head. "But none of that's important. What's important is you. And I'm taking a lot for granted. Did you meet someone while I was gone?"

"I met a lot of people while you were away."

"That's not what I meant. Did you meet someone special? I mean, should I jump out of this boat, swim back to shore, and just keep going?"

"No."

I heard a loud whistling, then a pop echoed around us. I looked up as the sky burst into color. "Oh, the fireworks!"

"Come here."

We shifted around in the boat until I was sitting with my back to his chest, his arms around me, the boat gently rocking.

More fireworks lit up the sky. *Pop!* Red. *Pop!* White. *Pop!* Blue.

"I love fireworks," I said.

"I love you." He kissed my neck. "I missed you so much."

I was as weak as Chelsea when it came to being with the guy I loved. I twisted around and faced him. "How long are you staying this time?"

"Until the end of summer . . . if that's what you want."

It was so what I wanted. "I have tomorrow off."

"Great. I'll be around. We can do whatever you want."

Whatever I wanted. Right now I only wanted one thing, what I'd wanted the first second I laid eyes on him again, what I'd been denying myself because I wasn't going to be pathetic like Chelsea.

I wound my arms around his neck and took exactly what I wanted. A kiss. Sweet, slow, perfect.

It was exactly as I remembered. The taste of him, the feel of him. Wonderful and right.

I thought I'd never get tired of this. I wanted it every day, all day.

He broke away, pressed his face against my hair.

"Ah, Jennifer, I was crazy to leave. I was just insanely scared, because I knew I'd have to leave sometime. And I didn't want to fall for you any harder than I'd already fallen. It was so hard to pack up and leave, but I thought if I stayed it would be worse by the end of summer. Because I do have to leave, you know. Eventually, I *have* to go into the army at the end of the summer. I've already enlisted."

I heard the desperation in his voice, the worry, the trying to spare us both a world of hurt that only caused more hurt.

"We'll worry about that at the end of the summer," I said.

Then we were kissing again, creating our own fireworks.

CHAPTER 36

It was almost two in the morning when we returned to the beach house. No evidence that there had been a party there. Everything had been cleaned up. We'd learned our lesson last time. The place was deserted. Empty. And I hoped that everyone had as grand a time as I did.

Dylan and I had watched all the fireworks, then sailed around the lagoon for a while longer before finally pulling the boat to the dock and heading back to the house.

"Guess you won't be sleeping in my tent with me," he said, as we stood outside the door.

"Didn't think you had a tent."

"I don't."

"Where are you going to sleep then?"

"If it's okay, I might just roll my sleeping bag out here."

"We have an extra bedroom," I offered. "Alex used to sleep there, but he got lucky with Amy."

"Any chance I'll get lucky with you?"

I smiled shyly, secretively. "There's always a chance."

We went inside and said good night outside my bedroom. And then I lay in the dark with the wind blowing in through the window and the ocean singing a lullaby in the distance. The house grew quiet. The way it did when everyone inside was drifting off to sleep, and I thought I was probably the only one still awake.

Then I heard a noise, like someone trying so hard to be very quiet that he really wasn't. My bedroom door opened. I wasn't frightened. And I realized that I wasn't even very surprised that he'd come.

I was glad actually. Happy. He was there. Just like I'd imagined for so many days.

He didn't say a word. Just came inside, closed the door behind him, and got into bed with me. He put his arms around me, and we snuggled close beneath the sheets. That was all. Just holding each other, wondering what tomorrow might bring.

Dylan was still asleep when I woke up the next morning. It seemed no matter what time I went to bed, I'd developed the habit of waking up just before dawn so I could have that alone time in the kitchen. Just me and my green tea and the smell of cinnamon rolls baking. I watched him for a while. There wasn't much light, so a lot of shadows still hovered around us. I couldn't see him clearly, but it was more his presence that I watched. The wonder of his coming back.

What did it mean really? He'd deserted his best friend, abandoned his plans to camp along the coast. He'd come back to me, for me. That was a scary thought. A wonderful realization. It made everything seem bigger than either of us.

I eased out of bed, not wanting to wake him. Wanting my alone time to try to figure out exactly how I felt about him, about our situation. He'd told me that he loved me. My heart expanded now as it had when he'd first spoken the words. I hadn't given them back to him. I'd been too scared, too doubtful, too unsure of what would happen if I opened my heart completely to him. Was he here to stay as long as he could? He'd said he was, but did I trust him? How could I even consider that I loved him if I didn't trust him?

Because I loved him, too. And that was crazy. To fall in love so fast and so hard. With someone who would only leave me again, eventually. He had no choice. So his leaving would be different then. He'd leave because he *had* to. The question was: Could I accept and live with that?

I crept down to the kitchen, made my tea, put the cinnamon rolls into the oven, and sat on the bench seat by the window and looked out on the bay. I could hear the dolphins yakking to each other. An occasional foghorn. It was serene here. And I realized that I felt more tranquil at that moment than I had since Dylan had left, maybe even since the summer had begun. Because he'd returned, and it was like he belonged here. Like the house and I and everything were back in harmony.

I heard a whisper of a sound and turned to see Amy coming into the kitchen. "Hey," she whispered. She poured herself a glass of orange juice and joined me at the table. "How did it go with Dylan?"

"He said he loves me."

"That's great, Jen."

"I'm going to let him stay here with us."

"That's cool. I'm glad actually. Now I won't feel so guilty about having someone while you don't."

That was so typical of Amy. When Dylan had been here before, it had never occurred to me to worry that Amy might be feeling left out. But Amy did worry about things like that. It was part of the reason that she had such an affinity for strays. She wanted to give everyone a home in her heart.

"I thought I heard you two."

With a yawn, Chelsea dropped down onto the bench beside Amy.

"Dylan is going to move in with us," Amy told her.

"So you decided to forgive him," Chelsea said.

"I don't know if there was really anything to forgive, Chels. He had his plans, I had mine. We hadn't planned on each other. I don't know if we were really ready for each other at the beginning of the summer. I think we are now."

"Love is so totally scary," Chelsea said. "How do you know if he's the right guy for forever?"

"Maybe you don't," I said. "Maybe you just know that he's the right guy for now."

The timer went off. I got up and took the cinnamon rolls out of the oven, placed them on the table along with the icing. We all sat there, slathering on gobs of icing and eating the warm rolls. It was strange that the summer wasn't turning out to be anything like I'd planned, and yet at this moment, it was exactly how I'd always envisioned it.

The three of us sitting in the kitchen at dawn, watching the sunrise, while we ate warm cinnamon rolls. Friends again, friends forever. Always there for each other.

I couldn't figure out why I thought I'd lost this. Because here it was. As natural as anything.

Chelsea chewed on her roll, a thoughtful expression on her face. Then she swallowed and asked, "I've had the main bedroom longer than I was supposed to, and Amy doesn't want to move into it, so did you want to go ahead and swap rooms today? You know, since Dylan is here, and it is bigger, romantic with the balcony and everything. I don't mind if you want to have it now, since I've had it for so long."

I slowly shook my head. My grandparents' bedroom. I had wanted it so badly, and now, I thought that I didn't want a room that would have their presence in it. It was funny, but I wanted a room that had become mine. A room that would become ours. Last night we'd only held each other, but tonight . . . well, tonight there might be more. Yes, tonight there would almost certainly be more.

"No," I said, "but thanks for offering."

"No big deal."

But it was. Because we were all friends again. Thinking of each other and what each of us needed more than we were thinking about ourselves and what each of us wanted.

When I'd come up with this brilliant plan for

us to spend the summer together, I'd done it partly because I was terrified of a future that didn't have Chelsea and Amy in it. If I was honest with myself, that was the real reason that I wanted us to have this time together. Because I was scared. Scared of what my life would be like without them in it.

But now I understood that they would always be in it. No matter how far away from each other we were, we'd always be together. That's what friendship and love were all about. Distance and time couldn't touch them.

"I love you guys," I said suddenly. "I really do. This is going to be the best summer ever."

"It already is," they said at the same time, smiling at me.

Like they knew what it was I was trying to say, like they felt the same way and understood. Everything would change in the fall, but so many things would remain the same.

I remembered my horoscope that first day when we'd come to the island. I'd taken an unexpected journey, after all.

"Later," I said.

I went back to my bedroom. The morning

sunlight was filtering in through the window. Dylan opened his eyes and smiled at me. "Hey."

"I love you," I said.

His crooked grin grew. I loved his smile and the way he held me when I climbed back into the bed, and the way that he kissed me. I was scared, I couldn't deny that I was scared. He'd be going away, but for now he was with me. And that was all that mattered.

And we'd make the most of every minute of every day. And when he left . . . well, my love would go with him . . . and his would stay behind with me.

But until then, we had memories to make.

For more summer fun, don't miss these romantic getaways . . .

California Holiday

BY KATE CANN

Rowan is thrilled to escape England to be a nanny in America. But when the job goes sour, where can she go now? California, of course!

Tropical Kiss

BY JAN COFFEY

Morgan doesn't want to spend the summer in Aruba with her boring dad. Little does she know she's in for a summer of sun, romance, and a little international intrigue.

Don't forget the sunscreen! Turn the page for more . . .

From *California Holiday*

BY KATE CANN

We go through into the kitchen. Sha takes Flossy to one side and whispers urgently to her, then Flossy trots sulkily out of the room again and comes back with a large, professional-looking folder. "Would you like to see my artwork?" she peeps.

Oh, God. *Artwork*. For a four-year-old. But hey—she's *talking* to me! "I'd *love* to!" I enthuse.

We sit side by side at the table, and I take refuge in the daubings and stickings and sketches that Flossy pulls out of her folder. They all look a bit too careful, a bit too controlled, but they're good, good enough for me to praise quite genuinely. "I love this cow, Flossy!"

"It's a goat."

"Yeah? So it is! And this little girl, she's so sweet—is she you?"

"Yes! At my *dance* class. Mommy—when can Rowan see me at my dance class?"

"On Thursday, sweetie," beams Sha, from behind the plate of teeny-tiny bits of food she's preparing. "She's going to be *taking* you—won't that be nice?"

Flossy clambers down from the table and starts pirouetting somewhat sickeningly about the floor. I force myself to coo and clap. Sha's smile is now threatening to split her face. At least I've made up some lost ground in her dwindling opinion of me. "Sweetheart, come and eat supper now!" she yodels, bringing the plate over to the table. Flossy clambers back into her chair, and Sha and I, seated either side of her, watch her eat. She seems completely unperturbed by this, as though it's normal to have two adults entirely focused on what she's pushing into her mouth. I eye the tiny sandwiches, apple quarters and raisins with hungry envy. God, I could do with some energy food. That salad I felt obliged to order at the café was nowhere near enough.

Then out of the blue Sha asks, "I bet you're feeling a little jet-lagged, aren't you?"

This is the first real question she's actually asked about *me*, and I'm almost touched. "Er—it certainly feels like way past my bedtime."

"Well—good. I thought—this being the first night and everything—it would be nice if you went to bed the same time as Flossy. So she knows you're *there*, next door."

Oh, *great*. *Charmed*. "Sure," I mumble. "Why not."

"I have tomorrow off. I thought we'd have like a—*training* day, if that's not too awful a word! Then it's over to you, Rowan. And I know things are going to be just *fine*." She does her horror-clown smile at me and I make myself smile back. Then we troop off to get Flossy in the bath.

From *Tropical Kiss*

BY JAN COFFEY

June, Aruba

He was late.

The heat was giving Morgan Callahan a headache. She looked at the long afternoon rays of Caribbean sun sliding toward her along the sidewalk. The bench she was sitting on occupied one of the few areas of shade remaining on the stretch of white concrete outside the airport terminal. Sun was poison on her freckled Boston Irish skin. She avoided it like the plague.

How much longer could he be? she thought, looking at her watch.

God, it was hot.

Morgan glanced over her shoulder at the sliding glass doors leading from the air-conditioned baggage claim area. When she'd stepped out of the plane an hour ago, it seemed like the entire population of Aruba was packed into that area. Now she knew why. The air was crisp. The white floors were shining. Even the green plants in the raised dividers looked happy and healthy. And cool.

But she hadn't stayed inside. Hobbling on her crutches and pulling her bags behind her, she had come out ahead of most of the tourists.

She knew now she'd expected too much. Wished for the impossible. She'd thought Philip might just be there to pick her up. Waiting for her.

Fat chance.

Beyond the entrance to the airport, everywhere she looked, the heat was giving the island that hazy, miragy look. She could see in the distance, rising sharply above the flat surrounding area, one high rounded hill with a little white building on top.

"Come on, Philip," she muttered, tapping her good foot on the pavement.

The sweat was trickling down the inside of the cast on her leg, and the itching was about to drive her crazy. Thank God she'd at least been smart enough to wear a light sundress. She lifted the limp blanket of hair off her neck. It didn't help. There was no breeze to cool her skin. She tied her hair back in a ponytail.

Behind her the sliding doors opened and she glanced around at them. A short, middle-aged guy came out. Straw Indiana Jones hat, khakis, a large untucked Hawaiian shirt. Morgan remembered seeing him on the plane. He'd been wearing his hat even then. He had a nose that looked like it had been chewed on by something, and the tan, leathery skin of someone who worked in construction or who had spent lots of hours in the sun, anyway. He also didn't look like he was too hot on shaving. His chin could have easily been mistaken for the butt of some aging porcupine.

She got a whiff of his cigarette smoke and immediately became annoyed. The last thing she needed was to have her asthma flare up. He saw her looking at him. He smiled and started walking toward her.

Great, she thought. *American girl abducted from deserted Aruba airport.*

"Bon tardi," he said.

"I don't speak . . . uh, Dutch?" she guessed,

not really knowing what language he'd just spoken.

"Papiamento," he corrected. "The native tongue of Aruba."

"You're Aruban?"

"From the islands."

That wasn't much of an answer. There were lots of islands in the Caribbean.

He puffed on his cigarette and pushed back the rim of his hat.

"American?"

Wasn't it tattooed on her forehead?

"Yeah," she said, glad that she'd spread out her backpack and luggage on the bench. There was no room for him to sit down next to her.

"Your first time in Aruba?"

Morgan wished she could lie. The way he was looking at her was creeping her out. His eyes were kind of squinty, like he was sizing up some ripe cantaloupe.

"First time," she said, looking off toward the road. Two cars turned in from the main highway, but neither came toward the terminal doors.

"Boyfriend picking you up?"

"Not a boyfriend." She kicked herself after

saying it. She didn't have to explain.

"Traveling by yourself?"

"No," she said right away. "Visiting family. Visiting my father. He lives on the island."

"Works for the oil company?"

"No."

"How about if I give you a ride?"

"No. Thank you," she said tersely, guessing that he wasn't going to be much for answering questions. Still, she thought, a good defense was the best offense . . . or the other way around. Whatever. "Do you have a car?"

He held one hand out, palm up . . . like he was checking for rain. "What kind of man would I be if I had no car?"

"Then why don't you go get in your car and get out of here?"

"You can come with me."

"No," she said louder and more pointedly. "My father is coming to get me."

She could tell he was grinning at her. He dropped his cigarette on the clean sidewalk and crushed it out.

For the first time, fear clutched at her gut. She was in a foreign country. The airport had turned into a ghost town. She had no cell phone. Great.

Porcupine Butt picked up her backpack and dropped it on the sidewalk, making room for himself.

He sat, she stood. It was like a seesaw. She grabbed her crutches and tucked them under her arms. She wasn't familiar with the airport, didn't know where the other entrances were, but there was no reason for him to sense her fear.

"Unda bo ta bai?"

"English, please."

"Where are you going?" He patted the seat next to him. "Sit down. Visit with me."

"I don't think so." She hobbled backward a step. "I like to be left alone. Please go."

"Pretty girl like you shouldn't be left alone."

Morgan's temper started to push past her fear. "I don't know what your problem is, but I told you I'm waiting for my father . . . and he happens to be a high-ranking official for the United States government. He's here in Aruba on assignment, and he has important friends in high places. Very high places." Morgan wasn't going to say it, but, from what she could tell,

Philip Callahan had spent his entire, boring, low-level, bureaucratic life behind a desk, pushing paper for those important people. "He should be here any minute. So unless you're looking for trouble, you'd better just leave me alone and be on your way."

The sound of a car speeding into the airport from the road jerked Morgan's head around. Immediately, her stomach sank. A new black Jaguar with tinted windows was racing toward them.

"You wait for your father. I wait for my nephew." Old Porcupine Butt was smiling as he got to his feet.

The driver revved the engine of the Jag. Even this close, Morgan couldn't see how many people were inside.

"Come with us?"

She shook her head and continued to back away.

As the car door started to open, she felt someone put a hand on her shoulder. Gasping, she whirled around and swung one of her crutches hard. The wood connected solidly with the knee of the man behind her. She heard him curse out loud and stagger backward.

Right away, Morgan had a strong suspicion that she might have aimed wrong. The young man holding his knee was dressed in khakis, a white polo shirt, and loafers with no socks. All in all, he looked too preppy to be very threatening, in spite of the continuing stream of muttered curses. She saw him bend over and snatch his sunglasses from the sidewalk where they'd fallen. When he looked at her, there was murder in his eyes.

"What was that for?"

"You grabbed me. It was self-defense."

"Self-defense?" he said, scowling. "I touched you on the shoulder. You weren't watching where you were going. You were backing right into me."

"You materialized out of thin air."

"I came out the side," he replied. "These doors were locked."

He was tall and had a nice build. Actually, Morgan was pretty impressed with herself for being able to knock him back a step. His brown hair was longish and straight. Handsome, but definitely too serious. At least, right now he looked pretty serious.

"It's not nice to sneak up on people," she said under her breath.

"I wasn't sneaking up on you. You backed into me." His green eyes disappeared behind the sunglasses. "You're not even going to apologize?"

"I'm sorry," she told him. "But it wasn't like I hit you intentionally."

She hobbled back to the bench, grabbed her purse, picked up the backpack, and slung the two items onto her shoulder. The strap of the purse caught on one of the crutches. She tried to unhook it, but the backpack slipped off her shoulder, knocking over the two suitcases like a pair of dominoes. As she reached down to straighten them up, her sunglasses fell off the bridge of her nose. She tried to catch them, but the purse—still tangled up with the crutch—stopped her. Morgan pulled the purse off her arm and took a step back, glaring at the items in front of her.

"Behave," she muttered at the tangled mess of items at her feet.

"You *must* be Morgan Callahan."